TO: Clyde:

Good friends & knowledge are instrumental in life

Hupclund

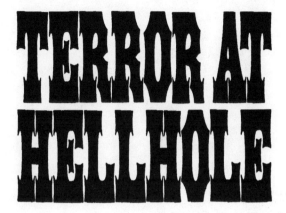

TERROR AT HELLHOLE

N.L. Terteling Library

Swisher Memorial Collection

AN EVANS NOVEL OF THE WEST

TERROR AT HELLHOLE

L. D. HENRY

M. EVANS AND COMPANY, INC.
NEW YORK

M. Evans and Company, Inc.
216 East 49th Street
New York, New York 10017

Library of Congress Cataloging-in-Publication Data

Henry, L. D.
    Terror at Hellhole / L. D. Henry. — 1st ed.
      p. cm. — (An Evans novel of the West)
    ISBN 0-87131-745-1 : $18.95
    1. Prisoners—Arizona—Yuma—Fiction.   2. Prisons—
    Arizona—Yuma—Fiction.   3. Yuma (Ariz.)—Fiction.
    I. Title. II. Series.
PS3558.E4977T4 1993   **$19**
813'.54—dc20   93-27133
                                            OCLC   CIP
                                          28634444
Typeset by Classic Type, Inc.

Manufactured in the United States of America

First Edition

9 8 7 6 5 4 3 2 1

To my wife Mary,
for her patience during the many hours it took to write this book,
and my sons David and Larry,
for their help and encouragement.

Yuma Territorial Prison
(1875–1909)

Across the placid waters from California's Mission Hill, at the confluence of the once turgid Colorado and Gila rivers, stands the grim remains of a walled structure known to early-day southwesterners, as Yuma Territorial Prison. But to those hardened inmates who were oppressed there, it was known as "Hellhole."

Within its rock and adobe walls, iron bars at one time caged the meanest assortment of murderers, gunmen, thieves, and cutthroats, on this side of hell.

During the thirty-four-year span of an iron-disciplined operation, history records that there were one hundred and forty attempts to break out, but there was never any record of anyone ever trying to break *into* Yuma prison. That is, until terror struck at Hellhole....

Prologue

In the beginning God created heaven and earth, and the earth was without form and void. And water was everywhere, and a great darkness was upon the face of the water. And God made land and saw that it was good. Then God created man in His own image, male and female created He them. And when Adam and Eve sinned, they brought sickness and death unto mankind.

But in the beginning, according to the Quechan Indians, when the water was everywhere and darkness covered the face of the earth, their two deities, Kwikumat and Blind Old Man, emerged from the dark waters.

Kwikumat was not satisfied with a world only of water, so he created dry land; and Blind Old Man, who wanted people, created creatures out of mud, creatures with webbed feet and no fingers. Kwikumat became sorely displeased with these mud figures, so in anger, Blind Old Man went back into the dark waters, dispelling sickness and foul air as he sank odiously from sight, leaving illness and death in the world.

Then Kwikumat reconsidered and decided to bring real people into being. He went to the sacred mountain of Avikwame (which is now Newberry Mountain, north of Needles, California). There he created Quechan Indians, and three other tribes. After this, he made white men and Mexicans on a lower order.

Life was very carefree for the Quechan people because they had no negative thoughts about bodily functions, nor were they ashamed of sexual relations. Their inbred lack of concern for material wealth relieved them of all mental stress, which plagued the rest of mankind.

Kwikumat had sexual relations with a woman of his creation and begat a son named Kumastamo, and a daughter, Frog. Later, Kwikumat sickened because his daughter Frog ate his excrement, but before he died he ordered his son to carry on the work of protecting the Quechan people.

After he died, the people held a mourning ceremony that was to protect them from evil. Then feeling shielded from harm, and contrary to their teaching, the tribes began to scatter. The Quechans gravitated to the Yuma area and life became much more rigorous because they had left their sacred mountain.

But these proud people soon developed an innate ability to ferret out food in order to survive the rigors of the merciless desert. And when a Federal prison was constructed at Yuma, they were able to utilize their inherent skills. Being immune to the searing heat and Spartan diet of this harsh land, they used uncanny tracking to return prison escapees for the bounties placed on them by law.

Cunning and tenacious, they moved like wraiths pursuing criminals over wasteland terrain where not even footprints were evident. Southwestern history records the Quechans as the greatest of trackers.

Chapter One

The sun beat mercilessly down on the two Indians lying among the rocks at the edge of the ravine. Shimmering heat waves distorted the greasewood and cactus dotting the land surrounding them. High overhead, a hawk glided in the cloudless sky seeking a late breakfast morsel but it soon discarded the idea of waiting for the men to leave the water hole, knowing that anything fit for a meal would not approach the water while the men were there. With a final sweeping circle over the oasis, the hawk winged northward for the banks of the Gila River.

Ho-Nas Good waved his hand to signal his companion to stay put while he advanced. From his position behind a mesquite bush, Palma nodded, watching Ho-Nas inch his way closer to the lip of the bank, his progress quieter than the tiny lizards moving between the rocks.

In the ravine below he could see two men kneeling at the small water hole sheltered by scrub trees bravely growing through cracks in the rocky bank. The stocky man raised a clothbound canteen to his lips and gulped thirstily, and Ho-Nas could see that there were only three fingers on his left hand. Dark-skinned, his curly black hair hung in strands over his broad forehead. On the ground beside him lay a soiled, trail-worn hat and a 44–40 rifle.

A large Negro, also on his knees, having just risen from ducking his head into the pool of water, straightened up to squint at the sun. With his shaven head, his wet scalp shone in the harsh sunlight when he picked up his rifle from the ground, then stood up to make way for the lone horse to drink.

From the description given by the driver of the Yuma stagecoach just before he died, Ho-Nas recognized the man as Hedgemon Print. The report had been that two men, one of them a black giant, had robbed the stage just west of Tacna, on the road from Gila Bend. One of the passengers reported that he had picked up the wounded driver's rifle and had fired after the fleeing bandits, wounding one of the horses.

Later, a dead horse had been found in the rocks five miles from the scene of the robbery and although great pains had been taken to hide their tracks, Ho-Nas was able to see that the two men had alternated riding the remaining horse for their getaway.

Tracking the robbers to this water hole had been easy while his partner was busy leaving a prearranged trail of bits of paper dropped along the way for Sheriff Waringer to follow. Moving slower than the Indian trackers, the sheriff's posse kept eyes alert for fresh dirt or disturbed rocks in case the thieves buried their loot along the way. This was an old ruse often used after a robbery so that if caught, no evidence would be found. Later the robbers could come back for the money when the opportunity arose.

Ho-Nas, however, was certain that the stagecoach money still rested in the saddlebags of Print's horse. He wagged a finger at his fellow tracker kneeling behind a small mesquite bush, signaling him to move out.

Tall and square-faced, Palma nodded his understanding before pushing his sturdy body away from the bank in a slow backward crawl. Rising, he moved silently away. Out of earshot, Palma broke into a trot, his fence-post legs churned toward the rocky outcropping where the horses were hidden. Palma was forty-six years old and an opposite of Ho-Nas's physical measurements, with massive shoulders and chest, thick-waisted and heavy-legged. He was also young Ho-Nas's father-in-law.

Not having the innate ability, nor the education possessed by his son-in-law, he chose to work with him as a tracker and followed his orders without complaint.

After Palma had gone, Ho-Nas slid his rifle slowly forward so that he commanded a better view of the two outlaws relaxing by the water hole. He positioned the sun with a quick glance, knowing that his fellow tracker, Palma, should return with Sheriff Waringer and his posse within the hour. He settled down stoically for the wait in the hot sun, doubting that the outlaws would venture away from the water hole until late afternoon.

His mind sorted through wanted posters trying to place the burly outlaw now sitting with the big Negro in the shade of a large rock. Then the name jumped into his mind—Jake Laustina. Three-fingered Jake, that's who the brutish-looking man was. Recalling the bold-lettered poster he had once seen in Sheriff Waringer's office, Laustina had been listed as an Austrian, a gunrunner, outlaw, and general badman with only three fingers on his left hand. Slope-shouldered and of medium height, he was two hundred and twenty pounds of bull-powered trouble.

Print and Laustina, armed robbers and murderers, he thought, a good catch this pair would make. He and Palma were in for a fine reward, probably get enough money to last him and his new bride for a long time. A thin smile tugged at his lips but his dark eyes never wavered from the two men.

Ho-Nas Good, generally called Honas by the white men who knew him, was tall, with a narrow face and hawklike features; there had been some Apache blood in his Quechan background. Young, he was not yet twenty-five years old, and he saw nothing wrong in joining the white man and his ways. Many of his people had fought against the invading white settlers, and as such, they were subject to sweltering in the summer and freezing in the winter, constantly forced to move between here and the Mexican border.

With the coming of Fort Yuma on Mission Hill, high above the Colorado River on the California side, the feud between his people and the settlers became more pronounced, and soon most of the contentious Indians were driven further from the river. After 1854, all the Indian land on the south bank of the Gila River was given to the United States, and Honas's people were scattered more than ever. Joining forces periodically for a raid on some secluded ranch or way station, only served to keep the Indians farther from the new way of life the white man was bringing, for the average Quechan's culture was singularly uninterested in accumulating wealth or property. Nor did they care for pottery or weaving generally valued by southern Indian tribes.

But Honas Good was not content to keep fighting and running with no place to lay his head. Tall and strong, even for a Quechan, he had no desire to be a leader among the tribe, but rather his dreams were invariably of worldly goods, dreams of wealth. And these dreams were strange, for Quechans ever since the early days had shunned wealth, but Honas was an unusual Quechan, and he envied the material comforts of the townspeople. He knew that a man could do much, even an Indian in the world of the white man, if he had money.

He would adopt the white man's ways and live as they did, vowing one day to buy his bride a real house, to take her from the mud-covered *jacal*, that hovel they shared in the desert with her father and mother. Here along the Gila River bank, life was easy for Honas and his father-in-law, for the two women planted their pumpkin and melon seeds, and, sometimes, wild maize. And when the river overflowed its banks, as it usually did each year, their crops were irrigated and they thrived.

And from May until fall, before the crops were ready to harvest, they lived on mesquite beans, which the women made into a bread, and fish from the river. Sometimes he and Palma would forage on the desert, filling the strong canvas sack they habitually carried with wild seeds or small game they were able to snare.

But Honas was not content with his present lot. Thinking back to the great drought that had swept his homeland, a drought so severe that not even their leader could produce rain or control the force or direction of the wind that blew the powdery dust choking the vegetation in the land, nor were any of their leaders able to acquire such power through a dream. He recalled how his toil-worn mother had taken him as a small boy and joined a caravan trekking over the mountains seeking food, until they reached San Sebastian. There he remained with the remnants of the tribe after she had died, to be educated by the kind friars at the mission until he became eighteen.

Yet in spite of the friars' teachings, he retained much of his native beliefs and these Quechan ways were still strong within him and his dreams frequently were about returning to his homeland. And when a particularly realistic dream moved him, the young Quechan bid the friars good-bye, and he struck castward to the Colorado River, then south to Yuma.

Torn between his Quechan heritage and his desire for a better life, he made his choice, asking Palma to work with him. He would willingly assist the white man in his silly game of crime and punishment for there was money to be earned at the high-walled prison and at the sheriff's office. Tracking down outlaws or bringing back escapees for the prison superintendent paid well, which was more pay than an Indian could earn in months of backbreaking work. Escapees usually left a path that was easy for a Quechan to follow.

And Honas almost always brought back his prisoners alive, which pleased the authorities. Bringing in live prisoners pleased Honas, too, not that he had a soft spot in his heart for escapees because of his training, but a live prisoner could walk while a dead one had to be buried or carried.

Hearing the raucous snort from one of the bandits at the water hole below, Honas's mind returned to his work. He eyed the sun again, guessing that a half hour had elapsed since Palma had gone back for the posse. He lay quietly, stoically, not taking his eyes from the two outlaws lounging in the shade of the brush surrounding the pool, listening to them argue with mild interest, even though the nearness of water caused his lips to tighten.

"Dammit, now I says we better head up to Ehrenburg. We kin cross the Gila an' be gone befo' that posse gits back this way," Print said, waving a long arm in the air. "Right now, I'll bet they's coverin' the water holes along Coyote Wash, then they'll go to the *Tinajas* befo' they start up here on the Gila."

A tight grin twisted Honas's lips because the big man was right, that's where the posse was heading; Palma was trying to catch up and bring them back. Too bad, he laughed to himself, that Print didn't know how an Indian figured things, didn't know that even now a Quechan was listening to him brag, watching his every move.

"Hell, Print, yore just guessin' that's how they'll go," Jake Laustina sneered. "Let's make a run for Mexico so we kin spend some of this money."

"Guessin' or not," Print growled, "that's what I'd do if I was leadin' that posse—cut off the water hole routes to Mexico first. I knows this land better'n anybody!"

"Anybody? Shee-it, them Quechans could find yuh even if they was blindfolded on a pitch-black night," Laustina growled. "But have it yore way."

"You're damn right, 'specially since I've got the only horse," Print snapped, eyeing his burly companion to see if there would be any further dissent. "All right then, we'll cross the Gila and head northwest until we reach the Colorado, then we'll follow it up to Ehrensburg."

"Hell, let's rest our ass for another hour," Laustina growled resignedly. "Especially if we got as much time as you say. With a little rest, we can go anywhere yuh say for all I give a damn!"

Print nodded, satisfied that Laustina had agreed. "They ain't no water 'tween here an' Ehrensburg so we gotta stay near the rivers."

Honas permitted his lip to tug into the semblance of a grin. Maybe, just maybe, he thought, the big man would get his wish. He'd stay near the rivers for a long time because the Territorial Prison at Yuma was located on a rocky hill at the confluence of the Colorado and the Gila rivers.

Behind him, he heard a faint sound and slowly turning his head, he was able to see Palma with six men cautiously spreading out to flank both sides of the ravine. Outnumbered and surrounded as they were, Honas knew that the two bandits would have to surrender or die resisting capture hopelessly. Neither of the men looked that foolish, and Sheriff Waringer was a man who would force just such an issue.

When all his men had crawled to a position at the edge of the ravine, the lawman gave a signal and the posse men stood up, their rifles aimed down at the two surprised outlaws resting at the water hole.

"What's it gonna be, Print?" Waringer shouted. "Give up or do we drag in dead meat?"

Hands raised, the startled bandits came slowly to their feet, eyes squinting at the many rifles pointed down at them. They were quickly brought up from the ravine.

"How the hell yo' find us so quick?" Print asked, disbelief set in hard lines on his shiny black face.

Waringer jerked his head at the two Quechans. "Honas, there, could find you blindfolded in pitch dark," he said, ironically using the same words Laustina had spoken earlier.

"Shee-it!" Laustina spat irritably, his angry face screwed up in a nasty sneer when he looked disdainfully at the puzzled Negro. "What the hell did I tell yuh, Print! They can smell horseshit an' tell yuh how old it is!"

But Hedgemon Print's stark brown eyes were only for Honas Good, and the livid hatred there forebode an evil reckoning with the hawk-faced young Quechan.

Sheriff Waringer took his lariat from his saddle and passed the loop over Print's head, drawing it up against his neck. "Clasp your fingers and straighten your arms," he ordered, then he ran the rope from the neck down to the man's wrists and tied them firmly together. He tossed the end of the lariat to one of his deputies. "Tie that to the saddlehorn, then throw me your rope."

With the deputy's rope he put a loop over Laustina's neck, tying the outlaw's wrists in the same manner. He handed the end of the rope to another posse man before he mounted his horse.

He addressed the two prisoners: "We're gonna take us a nice long walk back to Yuma. Keep your hands on that rope and maybe your neck won't get rubbed raw. You try to get your hands loose and I'll have the horses running, I promise you. And I don't think I need to tell you what'll happen to your necks."

The two prisoners exchanged glances wordlessly, then the big Negro's eyes returned to pour their hatred at Honas when the strange procession moved forward.

Yuma lay twenty miles west, twenty sandy miles sparsely covered with greasewood and dusty, gray-green cactus bleakly hanging on to the waterless existence. They moved slowly through the blinding glare of the brassy sun and the day's heat pounded down on the grim caravan slowly wending its way toward Yuma.

Somewhere along the way Laustina's hat had fallen from his head while he dragged stumbling feet in the dusty wake of the deputy's horse. No one stopped to retrieve, nor did he ask for its recovery.

Honas glanced across Waringer's saddle to find Print's eyes boring at him, saw dark lips clenched in hardened black cheeks. Pure venom blazed in the prisoner's eyes.

He looked at the hatless Laustina's face, noting the ashen-gray flush creeping over it in spite of the heat. He knew that the man was close to coming undone, that a heat stroke was near.

"Aaaah," Laustina cried. "Yuh shit-eatin' badge toter! Can't yuh treat us like men!"

Stern featured, Sheriff Waringer rode with eyes straight ahead. If he heard the prisoner's babbling, he gave no sign, nor did any of the posse turn or pay heed to the man.

"Yuh bastards weren't good enough to find us—yuh had tuh get these Indian dogs tuh sniff-shit at us. Yuh burnin' bastards, take this rope off an' give me a gun, an' I'll face all of yuh, here an' now!" Laustina shrieked.

Stumbling, he staggered before regaining his balance, then he screamed at the two Quechan trackers: "Dirty whore-born, red-faced scum! I'll git even with yuh if it's the last thing I ever do. I swear it, do yuh hear?"

Honas's dark eyes drifted over to Print. The Negro's eyes still blazed wordless hatred at him and in his heart he knew that the outlaw was thinking the same things as Laustina was mouthing in his half-demented raving.

But slobbering and ranting, the bull-like Laustina did

not break; his fence-post legs were still plowing dust when the group turned into the city street at Doten's Blacksmith Shop. And Honas Good was surprised at the burly outlaw's stamina. He knew that the man's hatred would be equally as great, and his vengeance as pronounced.

Back at the Yuma jail after the prisoners had been safely locked into cells, Sheriff Waringer called Honas into his office. He held out an official-looking envelope.

"Honas, I'm empowered to pay a hundred dollars for leading us to Print and Laustina, and the Wells Fargo people threw in two hundred dollars for you," he said expansively, "because we recovered seven thousand dollars from Print's saddlebags—Wells Fargo money that was taken from the stage during the holdup. Split with Palma anyway you see fit."

Honas took the envelope containing the money without a word, while the lawman moved around behind his desk and sat down.

"Don't know how you do it, Honas, but you always seem to manage to keep them alive," the sheriff said. "Now you take that Chato, he'd just as soon have killed them as not—and he generally does. Why, just last week he killed an escapee down by the river. Hear tell that he could've taken him alive real easy."

"The Flatnose Apache enjoys killing," Honas said. "Nor does he care that a dead man can't walk. I keep them alive so that I do not have to carry them back."

Waringer's smile faded slowly when he saw that Honas was serious. "Never gave that much thought. I only considered takin' them alive gives us a chance to punish them, make examples of them."

"Death is the final punishment, it needs no example," Honas said. "Nor does the same offender ever commit another offense. Why not kill them where you find them as Chato does."

Waringer tilted back in his chair, feeling satisfied now that the chase was over. "I didn't know that you felt that strongly, Honas."

Hawk-faced, Honas straightened to his full height. "There is great evil in the men you call Laustina and Print, an evil that only death can erase."

The sheriff thumbed his hat up from his eyes, a grin spreading over his rough features. "I'm glad that you're not the erasin' kind. The judge should be hangin' those two, an' no doubt he will because the stage driver died last night. But even if he don't string them up, you can bet they'll do a long term behind the Big Wall on the hill," he said matter-of-factly.

Honas stood silent, his young face expressionless for he had long since decided to play their little game of capture and punishment as long as it was to his financial advantage.

Waringer scrubbed a palm over the stubble on his loose jaws, then he returned to his earlier theme. "Too bad old Flat-nose is such a bloodthirsty Apache. We've already got too many bounty hunters who shoot first rather than go to the trouble of herdin' them in."

"That is how it should be," Honas said. "Perhaps Chato has his reasons for bringing them in dead."

"But killin' an escapee makes the tracker a judge an' jury," the lawman argued, "if he is allowed to kill any man he's after."

"Has not judgment been passed the moment a crime is committed?" Honas asked fiercely. "Who, then, has a better right to kill than the tracker who suffers the rigors of the trail, and who is consistently faced with death from ambush in the doing?"

Waringer took new interest in the intense young Quechan, then shook his head. "You're too profound for me to argue with. Anyway, I'm glad that you're doin' it my way, Honas. I'm glad that I can count on you."

Stone-faced, Honas nodded, then turning, he left the office, moving with soundless moccasins.

The lawman took off his hat and dropped it on the floor beside his desk, readying himself for the paperwork at hand, but his mind kept straying back to Honas and what he had said. Glad he was that the Quechan worked for him. Already there were far too many trackers who didn't understand, Indians who were too anxious to get their man.

Bemused, he shook his head. So far a few of them had brought in innocent citizens mistakenly, some of them even dead. And that got to be plumb embarrassing for a lawman. Then his thoughts strayed back to the hooded death he had seen in the young Quechan's eyes, and his mouth tightened into a straight line.

"I'm damned glad he ain't after someone for a personal reason," he muttered aloud, "an' I damn sure hope he's never after me."

Yet an ominous foreboding pervaded his mood as he settled down to work.

Chapter Two

Colorado City was founded in 1850 on the south bank of the Colorado River just west of its junction with the Gila, at the site of a ferry crossing. When the community grew, the name of the town was changed to Arizona City, and in 1862, a flood destroyed the mud and adobe structures. As more and more emigrants passed through the area, the town was rebuilt using a variety of permanent materials.

In 1873, the new community was named Yuma City, which is thought to be taken from the Spanish word *humo*, meaning 'smoke,' because the Indians frequently created smoke clouds to induce rain. Completely surrounded by the natural barrier of the relentless Sonoran Desert, Yuma City became the logical place for a prison—badly needed in a territory teeming with brazenly lawless men. Several other physical and geographical features assisted in making this site ideal for the prison.

The rushing waters of the mighty Colorado and Gila rivers added further insurance against escape. The neighboring Quechan Indians who roamed this savage land with a careless leisure and the instinctive latitude of a wraith, were frequently utilized to return escapees fortunate enough to have eluded the dangers of the rivers, or the stern rigors of the unmerciful desert. The prison authorities welcomed the assistance of these skilled hunters by offering bounties of fifty dollars for an escapee.

This arrangement, however, was not always as harmonious as one might imagine. Many Quechans made it a point to kill the prisoners before dragging them in, for older Indians like Palma still remembered with bitterness the impact of the Anglos upon their land.

Emigrants passing through the valley never had time to complete a single growing season and therefore they helped themselves to the Quechans' mesquite beans and melons, while their cattle devoured the grain and maize crops. When the Indians fell upon the intruders stealing their food, soldiers were sent from the fort; the army refused to consider that the emigrants were at fault, that the crops were not theirs for the taking.

When the Quechans repeatedly attacked the settlers for their depredations, the troop commander decided to mount a full-scale campaign against them. Palma vividly recalled the time when the army under the command of Major Heintzelman, reinforced by two hundred and fifty soldiers from San Diego, raided the Indian villages in an attempt to drive the Quechan men from the river area. But the warriors had fought back valiantly swinging with their large war clubs and sharp knives, killing six soldiers before they had to retreat. Later, forty dragoons under Major Fitzgerald tormented a group of Quechans moving their families; they pressed the Indians, brutally trying to make the young and old travel faster. The Indians had turned on the troops, and in defiance of powder and ball, attacked with only their primitive weapons but were able to force the soldiers to retreat.

Palma armed with a sharp spear, had driven the spear point through two soldiers, and had wounded three others during the fight. Unable to defeat the Quechan warriors, the army had retreated. Later, they adopted the tactic of burning the Indians' mud and brush hovels and their grain-fields, forcing them to scatter in search of food and shelter.

To make matters worse, the Cocopas tribe then invited the weakened Quechans to visit them, and while there, the Cocopas hosts attacked their guests, killing a large number of men and women, and taking many others as captives.

Demoralized, the scattered Quechans were never again able to mount an effective fighting force and had to content themselves with small groups of warriors who made limited raids on the settlers, or even their enemies, the Cocopas. While these warrior groups were not large enough for concentrated battles they were able to strike their foes by stealth, then flee before the enemy could recover.

Tall and blocky, Palma fought in most of these battles. Never a leader, he was, however, a strong warrior for his hatred against the enemies of his people was great. Then one day he realized that the Quechans' fighting days were numbered, and when a young warrior named Ho-Nas Good began to court his daughter Avita, he stopped fighting entirely.

Quechan marriage ceremonies were simple in those days and when Ho-Nas constructed a mud and brush house nearby, Palma did not object for he had already looked favorably on the young man. Soon Avita had spent four nights in Ho-Nas's bed, during which time he did not touch her, and then, because he had no family for her to prepare a meal, which was normally required to complete a marriage ceremony, she brought him home.

A deep mutual respect developed between Palma and his young son-in-law, and together they would forage the desert for food while his wife and newly married daughter planted melon and pumpkin crops in a swale south of Gila Slough. Spring floods overflowing their land provided irrigation so that their crops flourished in the rich soil.

"My father," Honas had said one day while they were out setting rabbit snares. "Last night I had a strong dream— a dream wherein we earned much money tracking down escaped prisoners for the superintendent of the walled prison on the hill, and for the sheriff in Yuma City."

Palma stared at Honas hard, not liking what he had heard but knowing that dreams formed strong powers. "I would never work for the white people," he snapped. "It would be unthinkable to work for our enemies."

"Then would you work for me?" Honas had asked. "I could deal with them so that you would only need to assist me. Because I have been educated by the padres of San Sebastian, I understand the white man and his foolish ways. And because we are Quechans, we are superior to them in ability to seek and capture the escaping prisoners."

Disturbed, Palma studied the hawk-eyed young man while he pondered the idea. What Honas said had much merit and he considered it. "But, if I do go with you, I will never seek another Indian even if he is a prisoner," he had said. "And I will always try to kill the white escapees whenever I can."

Doubt crossed his son-in-law's face. "It is better, my father, if we do not kill them unless it is necessary to protect ourselves, for the white man foolishly still has regards for convicts even though they have committed evil deeds. It is the way of their religion."

"Why is this so?" Palma asked, puzzled by what Honas had said.

The younger man shook his head. "This I do not know, but it is so. Our Gods are not like their God, therefore we do not have to spare our enemies. But if we do not kill the prisoners, our services will be in greater demand than for other trackers."

"Does not Chato often kill the men he seeks?" Palma asked, clearing his throat gruffly. "I have heard it said so many times in Yuma City."

"But he is an Apache with an inborn hate," Honas had answered, knowing the direction Palma's thoughts would lead him.

"I, too, have a deep hatred," the older man muttered angrily, sifting back through memories burned deep into his mind.

"You and our people have suffered much at the hands of the white man," Honas told the older Indian. "More so than the Apache because we were never as well organized, nor were we so cruel as they. Moreover, Chato hates all men regardless of race. He respects only strength and power."

Palma nodded sagely. His young son-in-law was indeed a man of wisdom, a man far more intelligent than other men of so few summers. "And what would we do with our wealth?" he asked. "The Quechan has never worshiped worldly goods."

Honas looked pleased, sensing that his father-in-law was relenting. "We will have warm clothing for the winter, white men's clothing, and dresses for our women. We will be able to buy coffee and sugar, and bright cloth and needles with thread for our wives."

Caught up in the desire to add to the list, Palma said: "I would like some tobacco and a good pipe."

"That, too, my father. We will soon have good rifles and knives that French Frankie will get for us, and steel traps that the merchants sell." Then Honas added firmly, "And one day I will buy Avita a real house in the city."

Feeling already committed, Palma sighed. Tired of war, and continually fleeing from one place to another, he decided that he would do it. "Then so be it, my son. I will do as you ask."

Honas placed a hand on Palma's shoulder. "May it always be so, my father." And the older Indian nodded in agreement, for to obey a dream was strong medicine.

They moved their dwelling and together they built a larger house in a clump of trees at the site of a little-known water hole, away from the beaten path. Soon they began to prosper by working together.

Tracking for the warden of the prison, and at other times helping Sheriff Waringer at Yuma City, the two Quechans speedily earned a reputation for their ability to track down and bring back alive the prisoners they had been engaged to capture. Only if there was a gunfight, did the two men fail to return with live renegades. Soon they were called during all prison breaks because they could ferret out hiding places undetected by guards, and the Yuma City sheriff always selected them for his posses. Only Chato, the Apache, could match Honas's skill to follow a spore on the blazing desert, but because of his inherent cruelty, preference was usually given to the young Quechan if he was readily available.

Honas led the group of searchers through the underbrush thriving along the coffee-colored river. Occasionally reeds grew out into the water wherever the swift flow had been restricted by sandbars or accumulated debris and driftwood.

Pausing, he pointed up the steep sandy bank and said, "Your man Ayala, this is where he left the river. He crept up into those bushes until he got past the outskirts of the settlement. Up there he can travel faster with less chance of being seen."

Palma nodded and spoke in agreement, "The spoor is fresh. He has moved slowly, staying in the brush until he was past the river people living here."

Guard Frank Allison scuffed the sand with a square-toed boot. He smiled grimly. "Guess you're right. None of the Mexicans or whites who live along the riverbanks claim to have seen anyone. It must have taken Ayala some tall hiding and sneaking around to get this far without being seen. That's bound to have slowed him so we must be pretty close."

The river dwellers, with their mud and brush hovels, were human outcasts who survived along the banks downstream from Yuma, existing on fish, competing with the many gulls that flew up from the gulf of California, for the debris that floated down the Colorado. Wood, garbage, and anything floatable, discarded by their more affluent neighbors in Yuma, was how they made their living.

Palma nodded again. "We can travel faster now and he has less concealment to hide his tracks."

Honas was the first man up the bank. Barren gullies fingered the baked earth sparsely covered with useless sagebrush struggling to grow. Inland, the far hills shrouded in a gray haze were barely perceptible against the blandness of the desert, a brown drabness created by centuries of sun and dust, and the eternal shimmering heat. There was nothing but sun-parched sand and cactus.

He raised a hand for silence, straining to hear the faint sound of the prison siren floating through the windless air. "Another escape," he said, looking at Allison. "If we're lucky they may come down this way, maybe even run right into us. Otherwise, Chato and Ben Harplee will have to do without us unless you want to give up on Ayala."

"No, by God." Allison held up his hand in reproach, his eyes straight ahead. "We'll keep after Franco Ayala. I don't want the little bastard getting away. After we find him, we can help them if we get back in time."

Honas exchanged glances with Palma, seeking his concurrence, then he agreed with a nod. "We'll find him soon."

The two Quechan trackers moved forward rapidly, stepping up their pace now that their quarry was near at hand. Desperate, because he had left the cover of the river brush, the fleeing convict's tracks were more visible for the ground had turned to sand.

Fear lent speed to frightened feet, but within that very fear, panic was beginning to enervate the escapee in this harsh desert land. Not the soft sand of an ocean beach, but rather an unyielding reflector of the scorching heat stifling his lungs. The specter of death hooded this inhospitable terrain that supported only scrub growth and deadly creatures; snakes and scorpions, lizards and spiders were rampant among the greasewood bushes, and always the irritating swarms of insects hovered over him.

Water was difficult to locate in this desolate region where a feeling of loneliness and frustration would gradually unbalance a man's mind. Fearful of towns, yet even more fearful of the desert with its mirages and afflictions, an escapee could, and often did, become a babbling, deranged thing beyond any sense of direction. High in the distant sky, three buzzards began to float serenely, occasionally circling as they were wont to do in their age-old waiting game as harbingers of death.

It was near the evening of the third day that the pursuers came upon Franco Ayala lying in a ragged heap, a slobbering, beaten hulk of what once had been a feisty man, a man who in his incoherent bewilderment had been drifting in great circles, staggering short of his goal of reaching the Mexican border.

Allison gave him water and some food in a slow feeding process. Then he placed handcuffs on him before allowing him a few hours rest. The four men moved their prisoner in a direct route back to the prison, arriving there in time for breakfast on the morning of the sixth day.

And it was a day long to be remembered for its anger and sadness.

Chapter Three

"I'm sorry, Honas," Superintendent Joshua Tarbow said. "Because you and Palma were gone so long, I thought it best to have your wife and her mother buried at once." He stopped his pacing to look at the two trackers before clearing his throat. "I thought it best because the women had been—er, assaulted, then badly disfigured."

"Assaulted, disfigured?" Honas exchanged glances with stern-faced Palma, waiting for the warden to continue his explanation of the five escapees' sordid rampage at the Quechan's cabin,

"Raped," he said nervously. "And both women had been cut many times with a knife." Tarbow looked pained, forcing himself to go on. "Your wife...they were both slashed beyond recognition, according to Chato."

"Who were the men who did this terrible thing?" Honas asked, his ashen face still impassive.

"The five prisoners who escaped were responsible. They got away by killing Guard Sheaves, shortly after you and Palma went with Allison to get Ayala," Tarbow said. "Harplee and four guards took Chato and went after them but didn't catch up until after they wreaked havoc on your place. They were an all-night work detail, so they weren't missed until morning relief. Harplee caught up with them just after they left your place. Their shackles were found at an old prospector's shed not far from here."

Tarbow paced back and forth, trying to read some sign of sorrow in the young Quechan's hawklike features, but with the exception of a light that now blazed in the obsidian eyes, no emotion was evident.

"Chato wounded Carugna, would have killed him but Harplee struck the rifle down just as Chato fired, knocking off his aim," Tarbow said. "If only he killed them all!"

Then he paused, looking aghast at what he had just said. He added, "I say this only to you; because of my position, I cannot express such thoughts to the public. But you know how honorable Ben Harplee is, he would not allow Chato to kill them. He even ordered Chato back alone, not trusting the Apache to help bring in live prisoners."

"Names, Warden, who are they?" Honas asked coldly. "I want their names."

"Print and Laustina, you already know. Carugna, Dwyer..." Tarbow stopped abruptly, a quizzical expression replacing his sad look. Noting both men's silence, he asked: "Say, you are not thinking of...?"

"Thinking of what?" Honas asked, his bronze face blandly reflecting light from the window. But the Quechan's dark eyes still blazed.

"Well, I—I..." Tarbow shook his head. "Anyway, the three were sentenced to life imprisonment by Judge Morcum the following day because of their earlier misdeeds. Dwyer and Powers were given an additional year to be added to their five-year sentence."

"These men, this is all the sentence they received for rape and murder of two women?" Honas asked, not comprehending the white man's justice. "This Morcum, this judge—he is as guilty as they, and he, too, should be sentenced."

Tarbow threw up his hands in exasperation. "Maybe so, but he's all we have for a judge. You should see how lenient he is when he's sober, but half drunk, he's impossible! Why he nearly threw the case out of court when he found out that the murdered women were Indians."

The young Quechan's jaw tightened and his voice was cold. "And if the women had been white, then what would this Judge Morcum have done?"

The superintendent shrugged, gesturing helplessly with his hands. "I—I don't know." Then sensing the Quechan's discouragement, he added softly: "I'm sorry, Honas. The tide of justice courses strangely at times and washes over us all. At any rate, they have been sentenced to long terms."

"It is true, they have now all been sentenced," Honas said coldly, and his tone caused Tarbow to throw him a quick look.

"Let it lay, Honas," he said, his eyes trying to find something in the Quechan's face. "You're a good man, so don't do anything foolish."

"I never do anything foolish, sir," Honas told the superintendent. "And you say that they have been given sentences that can be changed at the whim of any other judge?"

"Their terms will be carried out, at least as long as I am here."

"And if you should happen to leave..." Honas paused, then added, "Or if some other judge chooses to reduce their sentences?"

"W-well." The superintendent shrugged. "I'm sorry, truly sorry."

Honas nodded gravely. "Thank you for your concern, Warden." he said before striding purposefully from the room.

Palma stood looking at Tarbow a moment longer, his face void of expression. Then he, too, walked quickly out the door left open by his son-in-law.

* * *

The smoky coal oil lamp was dim. The fetid air inside the small back room of the clapboard shack would have been unbearable to most white men, but the odors were entirely unnoticeable to the three men sitting on rickety chairs at a crude table.

Located a short distance off the alley did not save the shack from the loud songs and laughter cascading from the open cantina doors; the sounds were nearly drowned by guitars and accordions. Raucous laughter and squeals of delight floated down from bawdy house windows, houses that lined the dusty thoroughfare of iniquity. This street of sin known to the inhabitants of Yuma as Rincon Alley, stretched from First Street northward to Jones. The alley harbored the most violent atmosphere in Yuma outside of the grim prison walls on the hill above.

Here, whiskey, drugs, and women could be had for the asking, while murder required only a few more words to seal the bargain.

Honas looked at the swarthy French half-breed sitting in the dimness across the table from Palma. French Frankie Coneaut was a man of great and varied talents, and an ability to ferret out anything salable. With an errant Frenchman for a father, and a Papago slave woman mother, he had a penchant for dealing in anything illegal, and nothing was too large or small for his notice if enough money was involved.

"I need a blasting cap and a short length of fuse," Honas told Coneaut. "And you will bring me five expensive cigars from the Colorado Hotel, the best that money can buy, understand?"

"*Oui*," Coneaut said, shrugging. "But it will cost you maybe a half-dollah each cigar," he said, then added: "The blasting cap is no problem."

Honas nodded, knowing that he had come to the right man for his needs. "I also want a length of very thin wire, such as is found in pianos."

"Ho, ho," Coneaut exclaimed, his little eyes widening. "Some piano wire, an' a fine garrote it makes, by God!"

The young Quechan eyed the Frenchman wordlessly, the angle of his hawk face shining strangely in the dim light. Getting no response, the half-breed arose from his chair, his face becoming almost lost in the aura of the dim lamp.

"*Mon Dieu*, it will take some more time to find what you ask," he halted, then stretched out his hand, "I weel need some advance money, by God."

Honas took two ten-dollar gold pieces from a leather bag tucked in the belt of his denims, and laid them on the table. "We will wait for you here."

Coneaut pocketed the coins. He waved a hand expansively around the room. "There is more brandy in the cupboard. My shop is your shop, *monsieurs*."

Palma found two tin cups on a shelf near the bottle of brandy after the Frenchman had gone. He poured two stiff drinks and they sat down to wait, listening to the cantina noises disturbing the night. Listening and drinking, they passed the time without talk, each man deep in his own thoughts.

Much to his credit, Coneaut had moved quickly, covering the distance to the Colorado Hotel located on Gila Street at the east end of First in short order. He placed the five cigars on the table in the dim light before he turned back to the door.

"Frankie," Honas called, and when Coneaut turned, he pointed toward the cigars. "Have one, you did good."

"*Monsieur*." Coneaut nodded his thanks for the smoke, sticking it in his mouth. He closed the door softly behind him and moved away in the hot night.

Honas broke a thin slat of wood from a packing crate, then, using his knife, he carefully whittled the slat into a long thin point. Then, even more carefully, he probed the pointed stick into the open end of the cigar, twisting it like a drill bit slowly until he had drilled a hole about halfway into the length of the cigar, tamping the shredded tobacco from the cigar onto the table as he drilled. Not satisfied with the hole, he repeated the process on two more cigars until he was certain that the hole was long enough and that the outside appearance of the cigar did not show any damage from the drilling. He laid the stick beside the cigars before he poured himself and Palma another drink.

The brandy bottle was empty by the time Coneaut returned. He placed a shiny copper blasting cap on the table, then from the inside of his shirt he took a twelve-inch length of fuse and laid it triumphantly beside the blasting cap. Then he stooped beneath the counter and brought up a small loop of thin, glistening steel wire and laid it on the table.

"*Sacre Dieu!*" the Frenchman chortled, slapping his hands together. "What is this about Indians cannot drink, eh? I return an' find my brandy, she is all gone, an' there are no drunken Indians." He waved his arms in an arc. "Everyone, say do not give the Indians to drink or they will be drunk. Here I find my Indians still very sober, by God!" he cried, slapping his hands together gleefully.

"Do not believe everything the white man says," Honas told him.

While Palma and Coneaut poured drinks from a fresh bottle, he cut a short piece of fuse and crimped it carefully into the blasting cap, then trimmed it so that only a half inch of fuse was visible. With steady fingers he gingerly pushed the copper blasting cap into the hole he had drilled in a selected cigar, and cutting a short section from one of the other cigars, he peeled some of the flat tobacco and rolled it tightly, then plugged the hole in the cigar, hiding the fuse.

He held the cigar up and inspected it critically. He handed it to Palma, and the older Quechan turned it around and around, looking at it carefully. Grim-faced, he gave it to Coneaut with a grunt of satisfaction.

The half-breed Frenchman peered at the tampered end, then sniffed at it deeply, noting that the strong tobacco covered the black powder odor. Nodding sagely, he handed it back to the young Quechan, and standing up, he squared his shoulders so that his posture became soldierly. Raising a hand smartly to his brow in a mock salute, he chuckled.

"Mais oui!" he cried enthusiastically, clicking his heels together sharply. "The condemned man, he smoked one last cigar, by God!"

The two Quechans exchanged glances but said nothing. The truth of his words would come on the morrow.

Chapter Four

On the last day of his life, Fishel Dwyer, morphine addict, sneak thief, and larcenist, awoke shakily when the prison guard banged his heavy key ring against the bars of the outer door. The cell was one in the row of fourteen single stalls reserved for incorrigibles and troublemakers. He was a fiddle-string taut, nervous man not given to violence, yet like a magnet, he was invariably drawn to trouble because of his insatiable need. Being a morally weak man, he found it easier to blot things from his mind with drugs or by smoking loco weed. But his immediate predicament was not of his own doing, but rather a whim of fate.

On the bunk across from him, Dalton Powers sat with his small feet encased in worn boots dangling over the side of his cot.

"Smile, Fish," Powers said without enthusiasm. "Our maximum-security time is up now, an' we're free as anyone in here."

When the jibe didn't bring any response from the emaciated Dwyer, he added: "Well, at least they didn't hang us even if the man said that we were accessories to murder."

Fish, as Fishel Dwyer was called by the other convicts because of his pasty skin and large bulgy eyes, was also given to spasms of twitching and shaking—body movements that he had manifested after many years of smoking opium, and now more recently, the easily obtainable loco weed, which was a product of the general area.

His long face was heavily lined for a man of forty-five years of age. It had been that way even before the rigors of three months in the Yuma Territorial Prison's maximum-security section for attempted escape and accessory to rape and murder. One hundred and thirty pounds of sallow flesh hung on his tall, bony frame. His pale, bulgy eyes watched Dalton Powers swing his small body, monkeylike, from the bunk.

"C'mon, Fish, let's get in the chow line before it gets too long." Powers nodded toward the open corridor. "You oughta eat."

"Ain't hungry," Dwyer mumbled. He ran a hand nervously over his balding scalp, his tongue swabbing at thin, dry lips.

Powers shrugged, pushing himself away from the grated-iron inner cell door. "You'd be a damn sight better off eatin'," Powers told him, "instead of always thinkin' about that junk you're takin' or smokin' loco weed."

Wordlessly, Dwyer watched the small man pass through the outer cell door to join the other prisoners in the corridor on their way to the mess hall. He doubled the thin straw mattress at the head of the bed, then piled his folded blankets on top in the prison's prescribed manner. Walking up the corridor he went through the cell block gate, then stood looking at the motley array of prisoners waiting in the breakfast line. All the men wore floppy-brimmed straw hats, with white duck pants or striped black-and-gray jackets and trousers. His mind wandered absently while he watched the men file inside the dining hall to their seats.

Suddenly, with teeth on edge, his hands began to tremble and a pain, sharp as claws, dug into his belly. Cold perspiration formed on his upper lip. Even after a month in an isolation cell, a time spent screaming and clawing the concrete floor as he lay in agony, the trembling still periodically seized him. Granted, the spells were not as long, nor as severe now that his body was slowly accepting his helplessness in getting relief, but today, standing here in the sunshine, the feeling seemed unbearable; the pain again gnawing in his belly.

He clutched the iron gate for support to ease his shaking body while his eyes darted upward, following the wooden stairs to the medical room above the cells. The city doctor who visited the prison weekly maintained a small office there—where he could find ample morphine to settle his shakes. His eyes swept the two north guard towers trying to determine if he was being observed while mentally measuring his chances of running up those steps without being detected.

Sagging against the gate, his pitiful body quivering, he knew that he'd never make it up the steep office steps, and this knowledge made him afraid.

Why, oh why, had it happened to him? he groaned inwardly. Just when everything was going so well, why had fate taken a hand? Certain people in town had been supplying him with enough loco weed to meet his needs, and when his urges demanded greater relief, two of the Chinese prisoners smuggled in sulfate of morphine for those who could afford it.

Gasping for a deep breath to steady himself, he leaned back against the open gate with a mild curse—if only he and Powers had not been assigned to that work group that disastrous day a long month ago. That was it, the work detail had been when his troubles had started!

Memory was a torrid thing bringing back that fateful day when he and Powers had been ordered to work in a group with Print, Laustina, and the demented Mexican named Carugna, to make adobe bricks just outside the east wall on the hill overlooking the cemetery.

He gritted short yellow teeth, thinking way back to that first moment when Hedgemon Print and Jake Laustina had been marched into the prison by Yuma Sheriff Waringer and his deputy. Standing in the hot sun, the other prisoners had looked in awe at the two men. Huge and hairless, Print, who stood four inches over six feet, carried his two hundred and twenty pounds of muscle like an angry, sleek panther, while Laustina, a half foot shorter, was as broad chested and stocky as a rampant bull.

Buzzing whispers among the convicts soon spread the word that the two outlaws had robbed the Yuma–Gila Bend stagecoach, and that the driver had been inconsiderate enough to die from the encounter.

A day of shoveling clay into a trough of water to be mixed into adobe blocks was backbreaking for a man of Dwyer's wan physique. His cellmate, Dalton Powers, although smaller, was wiry and much stronger, but the grueling labor under the hot sun took its toll in weariness on him, too, as they tried to keep up with the husky Laustina and the powerful Hedgemon Print.

Only Alexio Carugna, the swarthy Mexican, seemed to be unaffected by the brutal toil in the searing heat of the Arizona sun as the mixed mud was shoveled and tamped into wooden forms, then set aside to dry. Blocks that had been formed the day before, were now dry enough to move after they were taken out of their frames and stacked on edge to dry further. The five convicts had kept repeating the process from morning until night so that enough blocks would be available to extend the wall under an ever-expanding prison enlargement program.

The two o'clock afternoon guard relief had brought Homer Sheaves on duty with his rifle and the short leather whip he kept coiled and concealed under his shirt. A surly man with a deformed foot, Sheaves had limped back and forth while he kept up a scathing tirade at the five convicts, demanding greater effort from them. From time to time, he had snapped the whip, the leather strip biting into their backs unless they were able to dodge. And a fiery hatred was forming in their minds, a hatred that was bound to flare with violence before the day was over.

Shortly before sunset, the superintendent had visited the job to inspect the day's work before the prisoners would be lined up and marched back for the evening meal.

"They're dogging it, chief," Sheaves had reported. "I'd like to work these five troublemakers all night."

The superintendent had nodded. "If you say. I'll send down a relief guard for you," he said sternly.

"That won't be necessary, just send down some food an' coffee fer me, an' two lanterns," Sheaves had answered, jerking a thumb at the perspiring men. "Only some bread an' water fer them."

Later, the lanterns had been lit while night closed in on the sweaty, tired convicts. Sheaves took great delight in snapping the whip at the men as he limped about cursing them almost fanatically. Now that it was dark enough so that the men couldn't always avoid his whip, Sheaves aimed his snaps at the heads, laughing brutally at their cries of pain.

The moon had not yet risen when Print had worked his way silently behind the surly guard who was now heckling Carugna. Suddenly, he turned, and with an adobe block raised high in his hands, he crashed it down hard on Sheaves's skull.

Quickly, Jake Laustina had grabbed the rifle from the fallen guard's hand, and using it like a club, he smashed two blows against Sheaves's head and he fell backward into the shadows.

Then Print had raised a finger to his lips for silence while the five men listened for sounds from the prison to indicate that the attack on Sheaves had been seen.

"All right, men," Print said, "Ain't no one seed us." He quickly pointed at the two smaller convicts and had ordered in a tone that allowed no refusal: "You two ain't got no chains. We'll travel faster if you do the carryin'. Powers, you carry Jake an' my chains—Fish, you carry Alex's ball. Let's go!"

Jake Laustina, rifle in hand, with Print just behind him, had led off down the path toward the cemetery, Powers struggling to keep pace under the weight of the two heavy chained balls. Carugna, with Dwyer trotting along behind carrying the chains, followed in their footsteps. Beyond the cemetery, Laustina had circled the swine yard, walking wide around the slough, before coming back to the river. They made good time before the moon had risen.

Laustina signaled a halt, then in a low voice said: "They's a small place up ahead owned by an old prospector. Maybe we kin git a file or chisel for these shackles."

"Fish, you an' Powers sneak up there an' see what you kin find," Print ordered the two men without chains. "An' don't take all night."

Thoroughly frightened, they had crept forward, expecting momentarily to be challenged by man or dog, but nothing happened and they reached the open door of the shed. Fumbling around with shaking hands, Dwyer knocked a pail from a bench, the clanging sound rattling loudly as it bounced on the metal, scrap-littered floor. The two men had stood there with bated breath waiting for someone to come from the house.

"Must not be anyone home," Powers said. "That rattle you made would have woke the dead."

Evidently Print had arrived at the same conclusion because he ran across the open yard carrying the ball and chain, charging his bulk against the door, smashing it inward while Laustina followed him in carrying the rifle in one hand and his chains in the other.

Dwyer stood in the doorway of the shed, undecided whether to flee or join the fight if Print and Laustina ran into trouble. But before he could act, Carugna joined them, carrying the ball and chain over his shoulder. Then to Dwyer's relief, a lamp was lit in the house, casting a yellow glow through the blue-black of early morning.

His big band shielding the lamp, Print came shuffling across the sandy yard to the shed where they stood. The light from the lamp shadowed tools on a crude bench; apparently the owner did repair work when the urge of desert gold wasn't tugging at him, for Laustina had mentioned that the man was a prospector. They found a chisel, several files, and a hammer.

Holding his shackle against the metal hub of a wagon wheel, Print told Dwyer to hold the chisel. It took Print only four blows to snap the bolt holding the leg band on his ankle; then calling for Laustina and Carugna, he chiseled the bands from their legs as well, using powerful strokes.

Ransacking the house, they filled a burlap sack with what food they could find, then carrying bottles filled with water, they set out in a southeasterly direction, heading slowly for Mexico in a roundabout route, determined to stay clear of water-hole trails.

The first rays of sun were probing the Gila Mountain recesses when the five convicts came upon the mud hovel nestled beneath some trees that encircled the small well known only to a few desert dwellers. Boldly entering the adobe shack they came upon the young wife of Honas Good and her mother asleep in their own beds separated by a small kitchen area.

Awakened, the two women stood together in a corner, their fear-filled dark eyes watching the escaped convicts. Carugna wiped a dirty hand across his stubbly face, a smirk building on his wide mouth before he waved a gnarled forefinger, pointing at the young woman with colorful yellow ribbins braided into her black hair.

"I have seen these women before," he told Print. "They belong to those two Quechan trackers. This one with the yellow ribbons is Honas Good's wife, an' the other one is Palma's woman."

Laustina's head jerked up sharply at the words, and he exchanged surprised glances with Print. Revenge angled on Jake Laustina's heavy features.

"Well, well, ain't this gonna be a pleasure," he sneered, then he carefully stood the rifle in a back corner before he moved toward the women.

Print's eyes lighted and a white-toothed smile spread across his shiny black face. He reached for the young woman with the bright hair ribbons now cringing against the wall in front of him, ripping the gingham dress from her lithe body in one jerk, her nubile breasts quivering as she tried covering them with her arm while his hands sought the nest of black hair at her loins. Scratching with her free hand, she tried to pull away from Print as he lunged at her.

With a cry of anger, the older woman snatched a long knife from the table and rushed at the big man, mouthing curses as she came. Catlike, Jake Laustina reached out and seized her around the waist with one arm, gripping her knife hand with the other, then suddenly shifting his grip, with both hands he snapped the woman's wrist across his knee and the knife dropped to the floor. His coarse laughter followed her cry of pain from her broken wrist, then his huge hands disrobed her, ripping her single petticoat to tatters. Lustful eyes swept over her large breasts down to the hairy bush below the rounded stomach, and with a throaty cry, Laustina moved forward. Throwing her onto the bed, he mounted her savagely.

Dwyer passed a shaky hand over his sweaty face. Then he looked down at his trembling fingers while his other hand kept a white-knuckled grip on the iron gate. God, he had to stop thinking about things like that, terrible things that had followed during their short escape. Raping women, then slaughtering them in cold blood like cattle was not for him, even if they were Indians. His vivid mind still revolted at Print and the bullish Laustina having their way with both terrified Quechan women before disfiguring them with the butcher knife the older woman had dropped when her wrist had been broken. And his ears still rang from her screams when the brutal Laustina had lopped off one pendulous breast, or even when Print had slashed open her daughter's belly!

Callously, Carugna had insisted on his turn with both women in spite of their bloody mutilation, and he had laughed throatily because Dwyer and Powers had declined to join in their bloody orgy. Dwyer's stomach had churned and he gave a dry heave, glad that his nausea had forced him from the hovel before the real carnage had begun. Powers, too, had left the hut not caring for the bloody ordeal.

Then Laustina had hacked the two braids of hair from the younger woman and had thrown them out the door. "Maybe you two yellow bastids would rather play with them ribbons!" he called raucously.

Dwyer had looked at the blood smeared yellow ribbons before vomiting again.

Just then sudden fright brought Dwyer back to reality and he chilled when two shots sounded within the mess hall. Momentarily paralyzed, he stood still, pressing against the iron-grilled gate for support, his bulgy eyes following three convicts now dashing from the doorway, charging toward the main gate. Their leader clutched a rifle in both hands while the other two men held long kitchen knives in their fists.

Near the front gate, a guard shouted for them to halt, then he slammed the heavy portal shut before rifle shots were exchanged. The Lowell Battery quickly turned by an alert guard in the east tower began to chatter into the yard, bullets stitching the ground ahead of them like a giant sewing machine. Gravel spitting in their faces, the prisoners halted; now fearful, they changed direction and ran toward the prison shops off to their left before the guard in the northwest tower opened fire with his 44–40 Winchester repeater.

Mesmerized by the action, fright drew Dwyer's lips into a straight line. Detesting all violence, he sickened. When vomit began dribbling from his mouth, he ran for the safety of his cell. There he huddled on his folded mattress while the steam whistle mounted above the boiler room signaled a prison break attempt. Nerves grated, he covered his head with his arms, hoping to stifle the ear-shrilling whistle piercing the morning air. God, how he hated that sound; how much like the mind-curdling screams of the disfigured Quechan women!

More gunfire crackled during what seemed like an eternity but was in fact only a few minutes before the rifle-bearing leader lay dead with the other two wounded prisoners on the ground.

Calling on off-duty guards and trusted Indian trackers quartered at the prison, the superintendent entered the compound with his men to supervise marching the prisoners from the mess hall back to their cells.

Dwyer looked up when Dalton Powers strode disgustedly into their cell and flopped down on his bunk.

"Dammit, I never did get to eat! Them dumb bastards should'a waited for the changing of the guard, at least there wouldn't have been anyone on that Lowell," he grumbled. "That gun just scared the shit out of them."

Cell doors clanged shut and locks snapped into place while four Indian trackers combed the yard to make certain that all the prisoners had returned to their bunks.

Following Powers's lead, he staggered up and unfolded his mattress, then lay huddled on his bunk, his arms wrapped over his head to await the routine cell check that always followed an attempt to break out. He prayed for the wailing siren to cease, the sound rasped every raw nerve end, and he cringed in agony for the excitement brought the pain back to his stomach. He retched, then started to cough when nothing came up, and gnawing in his gut doubled him up. Perspiration drenched his black-and-white-striped cotton jacket.

God, he felt sick. If only he had something to soothe his quivering body. His mind swirled with the shrieking siren. "Damn that noise, I can't stand it! Why, oh why, does it have to keep going?" he whined in a broken voice.

"Hell," Powers snorted, rolling over and burrowing his face into his dingy mattress. "Don't you know that's just another sacrifice to the Great God Out." His voice sounded caustically strained as the high-pitched shriek continued.

Then the siren stopped, the wail fading off into a whisper before Dwyer took a deep breath relieving the pressure in his ears. He pulled himself up shakily, holding fast to the metal ridge of the middle bunk when he raised his head at the sound of approaching boot steps slowly scuffing the cement corridor.

Even with his back turned, there was no mistaking the big, dark-bearded guard, Ben Harplee, a tough but fair man. Dwyer did not, however recognize the Quechan tracker who walked along the corridor behind Harplee.

While the stout guard was busy counting the men in the double cells on the opposite side of the ten-foot-wide corridor, the Indian stopped to look through the double doors at Dwyer. Hawk-featured and dark, the Indian had a long, unlit cigar in his mouth and he stood there motionless as a statue. Tall for an Indian, he was slim, yet powerfully built, and his eyes, black as wet coal, locked on Dwyer's face like a candle at the bottom of a deep, dark pit, and seemingly touched the prisoner's very soul.

Disconcerted, Dwyer eyed the unlit cigar in the Quechan's mouth. He licked his lips when a chill passed through him and unwittingly he began to tremble. A dull pain locked on his guts and his face twitched as the quivering increased. God, if he only had something to soothe his jagged nerves so this shaking would stop.

The Indian took the unlit cigar from his mouth and his eyes moved from Dwyer's face to the cigar in his hand, then back again as though sensing the convict's urgent need.

Then the Indian did a strange thing. Silently, he reached a sun-bronzed arm full length through the outer door, then taking careful aim, he tossed the cigar through the inner bars onto the convict's bunk. And Dwyer gave the Indian a grateful look but he could read nothing on the Quechan's face before he moved after Harplee to continue the count in the next cell.

Striving to control his shaking fingers, Dwyer leaned forward and picked up the cigar lying at the foot of his bed. Quickly he looked over at Powers still lying facedown on his mattress. No use disturbing him, he thought, glad that his cellmate hadn't witnessed the Indian's gesture. For a white man, even a convict, to receive pity from an Indian wasn't anything to be proud of.

Holding the cigar in both hands to control his shaking, he studied it closely. He could see that the Indian's teeth had barely indented the cigar's end, and the smell of rich tobacco surged in his nostrils. The strong smoke would soothe him, help him overcome his agitated nerves, already he felt calmer. Yet puzzled, he paused, trying to fathom why an Indian would give him such an obviously expensive cigar. Maybe, in spite of the Quechan's inscrutable features, he had felt pity for him, and he was glad that Powers was still lying with his face to the wall.

He knew that it would be a long wait before all the prisoners were reported secured and that the sanctity of the prison had been restored. Better he should lie back and enjoy the smoke, knowing that the cigar would ease his shaking hands once the strong taste of tobacco coursed through his lungs.

With fidgety fingers holding it, he bit the end from the cigar and scraped a wooden match into flame on the edge of his bunk. Shakily, he held the cigar in his mouth and applied the flame to it. The fire drew poorly, and he sucked harder again before it caught, drawing the soothing smoke far into his lungs.

Exhilarated, his next puff was deeper but suddenly the smoke went flat; a strong acrid taste assailed his tongue. Then a blinding light flashed. Fishel Dwyer's face exploded and he knew no more.

Chapter Five

Joshua Otis Tarbow was forty years old when he became the superintendent of Yuma Territorial Prison. He was used to seeing death of every imaginable type but he had never been confronted by such a puzzling death as now faced him. He was chagrined.

With a slow shake of his head he arose from examining the almost headless body that had once been Fishel Dwyer. His shifting eyes were like brown agates sweeping the two guards, Ben Harplee and Frank Allison, and the prisoner Dalton Powers standing near the head of his bunk against the rear wall. The cell was small, about nine by eight feet, with stone walls rising to a high-domed ceiling.

"What happened to him, Powers?" Tarbow asked gruffly, anxious to have the investigation resolved quickly.

The little convict, his eyes riveted on the bloody mess lying on the stone floor, slowly shook his head and a kind of shiver passed over him before he spoke: "I—I don't know, sir," he stammered, then shivered again.

"What do you mean, you don't know?" Tarbow growled. "You were right here in this cell with him, weren't you?"

"Y-yes, but I d-don't know what happened," Powers insisted, pressing back against the wall, still terrified. He peered at the warden hesitantly. "I—I just heard a boom an' when I turned over to look, there he was, laying on the floor like this."

A light shudder racked the prisoner's thin body again and he finally tore his glance from the grisly thing on the floor. "I was layin' on my bunk facin' the wall, layin' on my stomach with my head turned," he whined, plainly frightened. "Then I heard this boom, an' when I turned around…"

"Did you hear him say or do anything before that?" Tarbow probed, a slow anger beginning to edge his words. "Anything at all?"

"Well, I heard Fish curse the siren. Said it hurt his ears," he added nervously. "I—I tried to humor him. Told him it was just another sacrifice to the Great God Out."

"Go on, let's hear the rest of it," Tarbow snapped when Powers paused.

The little man grew calmer; now his eyes were studiously avoiding the bloody body. "That's when I turned my face to the wall. It was only a short time before it happened."

"And you're sure you heard nothing before that?" Tarbow pressed on impatiently, his eyes frosty, a frown wrinkling his brow.

"W-well, I heard boot steps an' I heard the guard countin' men," he said. "You know, like after every prison break…"

Guard Harplee spoke out: "Yes, sir, I was counting the cells along the other side of the corridor first because there are so many more men to keep track of on that side." He waved toward the front of the hallway. "I was two cells down the line on that side when it happened, sir. I ran back here an' saw Dwyer on the floor like this," he said firmly. "Powers was still lying on his bunk, his mouth open in surprise."

"That's right," Powers rasped, pressing a hand against the side of his face. "I just had time to turn my head when Mister Harplee got here."

"Soon as I saw what happened, I just sent Honas to get you," the big guard explained.

"The Indian?" Tarbow asked quietly, his bushy brows almost covering his eyes when his frown deepened. "Was he with you all the time?"

Harplee's eyes swept out to the corridor and back again. "Well…yes. He was right behind me all the time."

"Can you account for him all the time he was with you?" the superintendent asked.

"Yes, sir, he was right behind me all the time," Harplee insisted, "but you know how Indians are—they ain't much interested in our housekeeping, nor counting prisoners, sir."

Tarbow pinched his lips together and was silent for a moment. He brushed his thoughts aside, too confused to pursue them from the evidence presented. But he knew that he must act before anyone panicked. He jerked a thumb at the little convict, then said to the burly guard: "Put him in the cell with Print and Laustina. Don't allow anyone in this cell except the doctor and me."

He let his eyes drop to the grisly remains one more time. "I'll send for Doctor Botts at once so he can do what's necessary here."

The prison budget did not allow for a full-time doctor, however, a small financial arrangement had been made with Dr. Rufus Botts of Yuma to serve as the examining physician and coroner as required. His office was located above the double cells and could only be reached from the yard by means of wooden stairs that were under constant scrutiny by both north tower guards.

In the corridor, Tarbow half turned. "Harplee, you make arrangements for a burial detail tomorrow afternoon."

Harplee touched two fingers to the brim of his hat in salute. He watched the superintendent edge through the double doors, knowing that he was a very worried man because the three prison commissioners wouldn't look favorably on such a death inside the prison. Especially not after the shooting during the attempted breakout earlier this morning.

He beckoned for Powers to come out of the cell. The little convict moved gingerly around the body, trying not to look directly at it while he shuffled out into the corridor. The inner and outer cell doors were made of heavy strap iron, and connected by an iron rod so that both doors moved in unison. This was designed to permit only one person at a time to ease through the archway, thereby slowing any speedy escape attempt.

"Allison," Chief Guard Harplee directed the other guard. "You stand watch on this gate. Nobody even looks, much less gets in here but the doctor, understand?"

Frank Allison nodded. Used to prison routine, he closed the cell door and leaned his back against it, his eyes idly following Harplee marching the wiry Powers to the end cell where Print and Laustina and Carugna stood, curiously trying to find out what happened after the muffled boom.

Irritated by the unusual happenings, Ben Harplee shoved Powers into the cell with the three murderers, and clanged the lock into place on the heavy iron hasp. His glaring eyes forestalled the question Print was about to ask before he strode away.

Print shrugged resignedly, biding his time. He would find out what he wanted to know from Powers after Harplee was gone.

Joshua Tarbow sat at his desk, fingers steepled together touching his dry lips. His fuzzy thoughts were gradually sliding back into focus, extruding from the stunned scene he had earlier witnessed in the blood-splattered cell block. He raised his eyes when the doctor placed his satchel on the floor and plopped into the horsehair-stuffed armchair.

"What's the verdict, Rufus?" he asked.

"I found a few slivers of copper in the upper part of his mouth," Dr. Rufus Botts said. "Copper slivers, they were, imbedded in the remains of the jawbone, and in some of the flesh scattered around the cell."

He paused a moment, sensing the warden's anxiety. "From the powder specks, I'd say it was probably a blasting cap that exploded and blew away the lower jaw and part of his throat."

Tarbow fidgeted with some papers on his desk, his mind striving to fit the evidence he was hearing. Then he sent a skeptical look back at the doctor. "You think he stuck a dynamite cap in his mouth and set it off? Why?"

Heavyset, florid-faced, the doctor shrugged, not wanting to commit himself. "I'm not saying that's what happened because who knows what a loco weed smoker will or won't do—or even why. Between finding the bits of metal and powder, there were only food particles mixed in with the flesh and bone. So you see, the only foreign material in his mouth were the copper bits. And because blasting caps are made of copper, and because there has been an explosion, I merely suggest this as a possibility."

"But how would he get a blasting cap in here?" Tarbow wanted to know, looking dubiously at the medic.

The doctor grinned. "I don't want to be facetious, Joshua, but how the devil did he get loco weed and morphine in here?" He gestured with both hands, palms up. "The cap could have gotten in the same way."

Tarbow's face went stiff, a flush showing that Botts had struck a nerve. "Hmmm, yes, maybe he did put a blasting cap in his mouth. Probably found it," he said halfheartedly.

Rufus Botts shrugged, knowing that under the circumstances, one answer was as good as another. "You're right, he probably found it in the yard. You have been blasting ino that caliche hill out yonder, haven't you?" he asked, purposely offering his friend a solution.

Tarbow thought he saw an out and he nodded speculatively while he reviewed what Botts had said. The cement-like caliche formation that covered the hill had needed some blasting to start holes so that sledges and drills could pound out the new cells needed in the prison expansion program. The plan called for additional cells to be constructed by carving out a new yard on the east side of the hill, which now formed the south wall of the prison. Already this wall contained the "snakepit" and the "crazy" cells.

His mind weighed the chances that one of the convicts had stolen a cap from the work area. He straightened his shoulders with a shrug; if the prisoners wanted to kill one another over some grudge, why should he care.

"You're right," he told the doctor. "The prisoner probably just stuck a cap in his mouth and bit down on it. That could set it off, you know."

"Or maybe he just lit it like a cigarette," Botts smiled in agreement. "He just did himself in, Joshua. Let's face it."

Tarbow nodded, feeling somewhat relieved. "Yes, I do believe that he committed suicide with a dynamite cap in his mouth."

"The man was a loco weeder, Joshua, we both know that," Rufus spread his hands with finality.

Tarbow nodded—the conversation had reached a convenient vein, one that was to his advantage...so why not end it now? He recalled that Dwyer had been a screaming wreck during the maximum security period following the return of the five escapees. No telling what a person in that condition would do.

He stood up, signaling the end of the talk, glad to complete the touchy discussion. "I wanted to make sure that there had been no foul play. I'm glad to hear your official determination, Doctor," he said formally.

Dr. Botts, too, stood up, equally glad to be rid of the subject. He gestured with both hands, then said, "No one shot him, no one stabbed him, nor was any poison found, Warden. I officially believe that he died by his own hand by some unknown means because his body couldn't stand the pressure of being without drugs."

Tarbow reached out and shook hands with the doctor. "Thanks for filling out the Circumstances of Death Report," he said. "He had no listed next of kin, so I'll have a detail bury him first thing tomorrow afternoon."

The doctor raised a hand in farewell and quietly closed the door behind him. Tarbow sank back into his seat and wiped a hand across his brow.

Chapter Six

On the last day of his life Judge Bliss Morcum awoke in a sour mood. Habitually drunk, this morning was no different from countless others. He sat with his feet over the edge of his bed contemplating the insistent rapping on his front door. White hair tousled, he gazed blearily toward the strong sunlight assailing his eyes from the window. There was no hurry. Anyone pounding on his door would stay there until he came. He belched, then arose unsteadily to his feet and began to scratch his paunchy stomach.

The knocking on his front door with renewed vigor. Clad only in long underwear, he shuffled to the closet and struggled into a faded gray robe.

Judge Morcum lived in a small five-room house just off Laguna Street, east of the blacksmith's shop. Already the leather-aproned hoof shaper was plying his trade. Morcum could hear the clanging of the hammer against the steel anvil above the thumping sound at his front door.

Moving ponderously through the living room, he opened the door in sour humor, but quickly recovered when he saw Tomasina standing there.

"*Buenos días,* sir," she said, her dark eyes staring boldly at him. The effect of that look shook him from his lethargy. "Today my mother is sick. I have come to work at you house, Señor Judge."

His bloodshot eyes dipped to the cleavage of her tight-fitting dress, down to the slim waist, then back up to her breasts stretching the thin material. Their eyes met again and a teasing smile hung on her red lips.

"Come in, Tomasina, come in," he said quickly. "If you'll excuse me, I'll get dressed."

Tomasina was the daughter of Manuel Lopez, who had years ago taken up residency with Concepción, a Cocopas prostitute. Lopez, considerably older than his Indian housemate, worked as a driver hauling supplies for Hooper & Hinton. Spending much time on the road moving freight, he laid no claim as the father of the comely Tomasina.

Bliss Morcum licked his lips, watching the girl sway past him when she walked into the other room to begin her work. In his more sober moments, he had watched her many times, walking along the streets of Yuma, and he had always gazed lecherously from afar. He knew that she was Concepción Lopez's daughter but he never dreamed that one day the girl would visit his house to work in place of her mother. Concepción came to Morcum's place each Friday to clean and tidy up for the next week's onslaught of sloppiness.

Good Lord, he thought, today was sure enough Friday, and seeing the girl, he vainly wished that he had been up and dressed before she arrived. He watched her move to the broom closet for dust rags before he went to the kitchen. He pumped a basin full of water, washing his face and neck and then combing the white strands of hair over the shiny places on his scalp. The feel of cool water restored some vigor to his spirits but it did nothing for the sour taste in his mouth.

Reaching under the sink he brought up an almost full bottle of Rocky Mountain Thistle Dew. Sloshing some whiskey into a glass, he downed its contents in a gulp, feeling the warm glow moving through his body. He took another long pull at the bottle before replacing the cork.

There, that was much better, he thought, a man needed something to steady him in the morning. He peered into the front room on the way to his bedroom, pausing to observe the girl's sleek movements as she dusted furniture. Damn, the way she wiggled her young body while she worked did things to a man.

Watching her stoop and bend drove him back to the kitchen and he took the cork from the bottle on the sink before he tipped it to his lips. Holding the bottle steady, he gulped until the level lowered several inches, the warm liquid filling the void in his stomach. He wiped the back of his hand across his mouth, breathing deeply, then he carried the bottle back to his bedroom.

Finished with her work in the living room, Tomasina came to the open bedroom door. Her eyes took in his ruddy complexion. Standing in faded red underwear, his long-waisted body, bulging stomach, and short legs created a ludicrous spectacle, and the girl laughed.

"I am ready to work in you bedroom now," she said, her chin inclined slightly, the saucy look back on her face.

"Of course, my dear, come in," he said, and when the girl started past him, he grasped her shoulders, drawing her hungrily against him.

Amused, she allowed him to kiss her, even permitted him to clumsily fumble with her breasts, and when she tilted her head back, excitement lay in her looks until his whiskey-soaked breath flung into her face. Stifling, she turned up her nose, but he tried to pull her toward the bed.

Her teasing mood left her and she laughed at him in disdain. He staggered when she pulled quickly away from him, laughing all the harder, but his hand caught at the neck of her dress ripping away part of the shoulder seams. Then anger spread its dark flush on her cheeks; her eyes ablaze, she spat in his face.

"Bastardo!"

Incensed, Bliss Morcum slashed the back of his hand across her mouth. "You filthy little Indian whore!"

"*Tonto bastardo!*" She shrieked, her breasts showing the lift and fall of her angry breathing. Spitting at him again, she ran from the house.

Red rage flushed over him as he wiped a hand across the spittle on his cheeks while he stood helplessly watching her run across the street toward the fiesta grounds. Her nubile body filled with animal magnetism had gripped him—hard! And the thought of this lush creature escaping him unsettled his drunken complacency.

Then he turned his bleary-eyed look back to the faded mirror over the worn bureau. They say that mirrors don't lie, but the man who Bliss Morcum saw hadn't been on this side of the glass for over twenty years. Earlier in his life while at Tucson, when he was still a mediocre lawyer, he had defended an Indian girl against the charge of assault on another woman over the favors of a gambling man.

Being penniless, she paid him with her body by moving into his flat, and pay him she did indeed, for her sexual talent made him deliriously happy. But just when he was falling in love with her dusky appearance and lush body, she ran away with a traveling man—a perfume drummer with a flair for charming women.

Wounded in spirit to think that any woman would prefer a salesman over an up-and-coming lawyer, he took to drinking. And all the while he nurtured a deep hatred againt Indian women, yet subconsciously he envisioned her talents to all Indian females, lusting for them, yet openly hating them, too. And still he continued his search, even though most of his sex was only in his whiskey-sotted mind. And so it was with his desire for Tomasina.

What was wrong with her anyway? he asked himself. Maybe he was a lot older than her, but by damn he was somebody! He wasn't like those callow young Mexicans or

Indian scum she rolled with every night. Didn't she realize that he was a judge and far above those worthless, loud-mouthed cowboys who called suggestive things to her when she walked down the street, trying to make her blush.

Just let her wait and see, he railed to himself, just wait until she ended up in one of those whorehouses on Rincon Alley, then he'd fix her, by damn! The first time anyone complained against her, he'd see that she was sentenced to the women's yard up on the hill. Maybe he'd sentence her to six months, then she'd remember him!

Damn her—damn all Indian whores! Unexplainably, it was always so in Morcum's dealings with Indian prostitutes, nor could he understand the insatiable urge he had for Indian women. Damn them, damn them all!

He belched, then stumbled over to where the bottle stood on the dresser. By damn, he had been glad to hear that the two women murdered by those five convicts last month were Indian. Raped they were—that's what should happen to all Indian whores!

He belched again, then struck his chest lightly with his fist to help dispel the knot that always formed when he became upset. Gas in his stomach, he grimaced; damn, he better calm down. No use getting so worked up over nothing.

Calmer now, he thought how first he would have sentenced the Negro Print and the barrel-chested Laustina to hang for their part in raping and mutilating the two women. But when Sheriff Waringer had pointed out that the women were Quechan Indians, a barrier had closed in his mind, and his heart had hardened. And he was sorely tempted to dismiss the case but only the fact that he had earlier sentenced two of the men for killing a stagecoach driver had deterred him from acting so foolishly.

Savagely he pulled the cork from the bottle and began to gulp its contents, nor did he stop until the bottle was empty.

He burped, spitefully rolling the empty bottle under the bed with a curse. Let that damn squaw mother of Tomasina crawl under and drag it out.

His rage subsided as he glared around the room. Better he put on his clothes and get out of here, he thought. Dressing slowly because he was having difficulty standing, Bliss Morcum finally staggered out to the kitchen sink. He splashed cool water over his face and dried himself carefully with a soiled towel hanging over the kitchen chair.

Noonday heat struck him like a furnace when he stepped out into the yard. He walked to the corner of Gila Street and stood for a moment, his frowning glance roving back and forth across the fiesta grounds toward the Chinese gardens, then he walked westward along Third Street until he reached the courthouse.

Inside the quiet interior, he loosened his collar and sat back in his chair to wait. At one o'clock, Sheriff Waringer stuck his head in the door; seeing the judge, he entered and approached the bench.

"Nothing's on the court agenda today, Judge," Waringer said. There was obviously no love lost between them but the lawman always kept his words polite.

"By damn, we can't keep this town going unless you arrest more people," Morcum growled irascibly. "Fines is what pays for things around here!"

"Fines pay for your drinks, you mean," Waringer said, a tenseness showing around his mouth, but he held his temper. "I'm trying to keep this town quiet, Judge, not trying to keep you in whiskey."

Morcum glared at the tall lawman, stifling words forming in his throat. No use making Waringer too mad, he thought. Might need him for a favor one of these days. And he had to admit that the sheriff was a reliable man.

"If there's nothing further, I'll be leaving," Waringer told him. "I've got my rounds to make."

Morcum threw him a poisonous glance, then tilted his head back against his chair, staring at the ceiling. Stuffy damn sheriff, who did he think he was?

Heat and the still air pressed against his listless mind and he soon began to doze, his sonorous breathing vied with the drowning flies winging aimlessly around the gloomy courtroom while he slept.

Stark sunlight burning through the west windows penetrated his befuddled mind, awakening him. He sat up, painfully aware of a crimp in his neck from the long nap in such an awkward position. He arose and stamped stiffly around his bench, shaking the kinks from his sedentary body. God, his mouth was dry and his tongue felt as furry as a caterpillar!

The sun was an orange ball balanced above the distant hills when he walked outside. Shirt wet with perspiration under his black coat, he plodded two blocks northward on Main Street, eyes straight ahead, not deigning to notice anyone. Turning east on First Street he could see the Colorado Hotel at the end of the block. Carriages and buggies were already lined up in front of the hotel for the hour of the evening meal was at hand.

The Colorado Hotel was really more elegant than his finances would allow, yet just being there made him feel important, and ofttimes he was able to cozen drinks from visitors and newcomers by overstating his importance. Whiskey drummers and salesmen were his designated marks, and he unhesitatingly milked them at every opportunity.

The barroom was crowded when he entered, and hat in hand he made his way toward a corner table when he noted three men preparing to leave. Hesitating briefly until the men moved from the table, he quickly slid into one of the seats, dropping his hat on one of the other chairs to discourage company. He reached for the almost full bottle of whiskey still on the table and possessively poured himself a drink, using the nearest glass left by the men. Then he poured whiskey in each of the other two glasses in front of the vacant chairs. Settling back comfortably in his seat, he sipped deeply from his drink.

A waiter, dressed in a white jacket, arrived at the table and Morcum quickly drew himself up, assuming his most dignified air.

"Leave the bottle, my good man, the other gentlemen had to step out on business but they'll return shortly," he said. With a flourish, he placed a half-dollar on the waiter's tray. "We'll call if we need anything else."

And the unsuspecting waiter, remembering only that there had been three men at the table, nodded, then strode away to attend to other customers.

A self-satisfied smile formed on Morcum's flushed face while he refilled his glass, and not wanting to leave the bottle of expensive whiskey he was preparing to usurp, he decided to forgo eating. He helped himself generously from the liquor as the evening wore on, and by eleven o'clock the bottle was empty and Bliss Morcum was drunk.

The crowd was beginning to thin out so he prepared to leave because it was imperative that he depart while there were still customers milling around or he'd end up paying for the bottle of whiskey. Picking up his hat, he quickly drank the other two glasses of whiskey he had poured earlier, then he wobbled his way toward the lobby.

The waiter intercepted him, check in hand. "The whiskey, sir?" he asked politely.

Morcum screwed an eye back toward the barroom where a man had stopped at a table to converse with some friends. He pointed boldly at the stranger. "Ah, yes, my good man," he said congenially. "My friend there will pay for the drinks and your excellent service, sir. I'm sure there will be a fine tip for you as well."

He staggered rapidly toward the door leaving the waiter to stand at the counter until his customer was done with his conversation. Outside, he drew a deep breath, pleased with his success. A storm was brewing and dark clouds crowded each other as a prelude to rain. The thin crescent moon could only be seen at intervals through the roiling clouds.

A streak of lightning zigzagged down the middle of the dim street, and dull thunder rolled overhead. Another spurt of lightning lit the intersection at Second Street, and he saw two gray figures standing on each side of the road. He blinked his eyes hard until he could make out their ominous shapes in the dark, blocking his path. Tall they were, dark and silent they stood, and a twinge of fear touched his spine, for one of the shadows carried a large war club and the other held a ceremonial spear.

"Who are you?" he cried. "Speak up! I'll have you know I'm Judge Morcum!"

There was no answer, no did either figure move. Another crinkle of heat lightning framed them in the gray light for a moment.

"S-speak up, you hear?" and when there was no answer, he tried again: "W-what do you want?"

The dark shapes remained silent and a grim foreboding touched him like a cold hand. His eyes, darted right and left, but nothing presented itself.

Maybe, he thought, if he walked away they'd let him alone, maybe they wouldn't bother him. He angled off to his left toward a darkened house as fast as his whiskey-wobbly legs would go. He reached the back of the house in safety, then staggered along the fringe of the hill. By keeping in this direction he would pass behind the blacksmith's shop on Laguna Street and arrive at his own backyard. The path was rocky and he stumbled several times, falling to his knees in his haste. He looked back, straining his eyes but he saw nothing, nor were there any sounds that he was being followed.

He dusted off his trousers. Probably just his imagination, he thought, or maybe a couple of cowboys standing out in the dark street. Somewhat relieved, he started homeward again along the base of the hill.

The storm evidently was passing without dropping any rain and the lightning was dissipating in its wake. A flash lit up the distant sky, and his heart almost stopped for the two specters were now standing twenty feet ahead of him. With a strangled cry, he started to run up the slope, slipping and sliding, scrambling on all fours he labored up the hill until he reached an old picket fence. Clutching the railing for support, he gulped air into pumping lungs while he listened for sounds of pursuit in the dark night.

Suddenly he realized that the fence he was clinging to was part of the cemetery located on the hill behind the blacksmith's shop, and that below lay the safety of his own home. But heart pounding, sweat pouring profusely from his whiskey-sodden body, he was again aware of the dark specters moving ominously toward him, their weapons held menacingly in front of them.

Cringing, he moved with his back along the fence, his hands feeling the way along the wooden pickets as he went. He paused at the open gateway, his heart thumping in his chest in abject fear when one of the dark specters appeared directly in front of him. Terrified, Morcum's eyes darted to the right, seeing the black shape of the second figure. Mouth agape, he backed through the cemetery gateway, moving backward until he bumped a wooden grave-marker. Still peering toward the dark figures, he backed sideways until he stumbled against a mound of another grave, falling to his knees.

He raised his glance toward the pathway, now hearing footsteps where before there had been none. What sort of devils were these? Morcum cried out in panic: "Who are you? L-leave me alone—please!"

But the footsteps kept coming, slowly, precisely, as inexorably as judgment day. Heart palpitating fiercely, he scrambled to his feet, eyes searching the night for a place to hide, but it was too dark. Then footsteps crunched to his right, joining the sounds in front of him as they herded him farther into the cemetery.

Terrified, he sought to cry out for help but fear had constricted his vocal cords and he was only able to whimper hoarsely. He turned and ran, stumbling, bulling his way among the wooden markers in his haste.

With his breath coming in great wheezing gulps, his body completely enervated, he was forced to stop. He heard the gravel crunch on both sides of him, felt dark fingers snatching lightly at his clothing, weapons prodding him to move. And then it suddenly came to him that these devils were purposely herding him toward some specific place; in stark terror to escape, he began to run backward.

Suddenly the ground beneath his feet was gone, and he dashed headlong, six feet down into the rectangular pit. His backward thrust and the force of gravity combined to drive his paunchy body downward and he landed on the back of his head. His neck snapped with an audible sound and dust rose from the grave as sand trickled in on the body that once was Bliss Morcum.

And the cemetery was silent save for the shuffling whisper of Quechan moccasins moving quickly down the hill toward Rincon Alley.

Chapter Seven

On the last day of his life Dalton Powers was already awake before the guard came walking down the corridor clanging his keys against the cell doors. All night long visions of Dwyer's faceless body had moved sickeningly through his dreams, disturbing his rest.

Built like a jockey, his scant four inches over a five-foot frame carried a slim one hundred and eighteen pounds, but recent fear and worry had peaked his weasel face. His cell mates began stirring. Now wide awake from the rattling of the keys, he watched Three-fingered Jake Laustina rise up to needle the guard.

"Hey, Allison, one of these days I'm gonna jam them damn keys down yore throat so hard they'll stick out yore ass everytime you open yore mouth," he jibed.

Easygoing, the brown-uniformed guard, Frank Allison, snorted. "Better you say 'Sir' before you try it because you're gonna need someone to help pick you out of the mud."

"Shee-it," Laustina smirked, reaching for his pants hanging from a peg on the wall. "You'll never…"

"Hold it, Jake!" Print cried, then he admonished the three-fingered convict. "Don't be gittin' them guards riled. We got us enough troubles without thet, an' smart-assin' will do it!" Carugna glared through the bars but agreed with Hedgemon.

The four men finished dressing in silence while the guard made his run up the other side of the stone-walled corridor. But it was Hedgemon Print who broke the silence. He scowled deeply before questioning Powers.

"How you think thet damn Fish git his hands on somethin' to kill hisself like thet?" he growled, awaiting an answer from the little convict.

Powers shook his head. "I never saw nothin'—just heard the explosion."

"Thet junker must'a gotten a blastin' cap from one of the workmen in the yard," Laustina said.

"Naw, none of the prisoners was allowed to git near them civilians who done the blastin'," Print told them. "But maybe he did find one thet got lost out there."

Laustina shook his head. "Them caps is too dangerous, they don't jest git lost," he said, shrugging his burly shoulders, and adding: "Hell, what's the difference—thet junker jest blew his damn fool head off, is all!"

Print wrinkled his brow speculatively. "Think maybe he did it on purpose? Maybe he was out to git one of us an' somethin' went wrong. You know we was always ridin' him perty hard."

"Who the hell knows," Laustina snapped, "or even gives a shit what thet silly bastid done. Let's git in the chow line." He slid from his bunk and strode to the door.

Powers followed his three cell mates through the short archway to the corridor after watching them squeeze through the double gates. Content to follow them, he didn't much care to be in their company, knowing that each was hair-triggered and highly capable of killing anyone who angered them. Their kind would even kill a comrade over anything that might benefit them in the least. And it had always been so with the low caliber of men he had known.

Years ago, while he was growing up, he had discovered that he would have a tough row to hoe because of his size, his jockey's body. Through each of his tormented years, he'd had to fight off every bully in town. And as he grew older, the bullies seemed to get bigger and stronger until he had became so bruised and pounded that he gave up fighting, and decided to stay healthy by his wits alone. One thing he had learned for sure was to keep away from the toughs, and when that wasn't possible, he made it a point always to agree with them. This often ran him afoul with the law, but at least he took less bumps and bruises by doing so.

But this fact had also been the cause of his recent trouble because he hadn't wanted to join the escape, at least not with killers like Print and Laustina. From the very start, right after Print had smashed the adobe block over Homer Sheaves's head, he had sensed that Fish Dwyer had been an unwilling victim like himself and had been too frightened object. He meant to side with Dwyer whenever he could safely do so, but the chances had been infrequent.

The other man in the group, Alexio Carugna, had turned out to be just another foul-mouthed devil, and Powers had decided to stay clear of him as well as the others. He shuddered, thinking back to the blood-spattered adobe hovel, and the bloody orgy the outlaws had enjoyed, the raping and mutilating of the Quechan women.

He brushed a hand across his chest. The striped prison clothes were now sticking to his perspiring body and he stopped walking to lean against the wall, pale and trembling, paralyzed with the effort it took to keep from screaming. And through his present fright, he remembered that Dwyer, too, had recoiled from taking part in the grisly affair. He swallowed uncomfortably, using the flat of his hands to push away from the corridor wall he had unwittingly been leaning against to keep from sagging.

Stark reality primed his mind; was this why Dwyer had killed himself—was it remorse or disgust? A tense grayness settled over his features and he tried to shake off this sordid feeling. Then putting all thoughts aside, he forced his feet to move, hurrying to the mess hall before the door was closed against latecomers.

At work call after breakfast, the four men were ordered to assemble at the tool room. Then, armed with shovels, sledges, and drillbits, a mustached guard known only as Hack, marched them to the southeast corner of the yard where several holes had been blasted into the caliche wall.

"All right, you men," Hack informed them. "Today you're gonna dig out another cell in this wall." He pointed with his rifle barrel toward the corner of the yard. "You're also gonna dig a gateway alongside that east wall."

"A gateway?" Laustina snorted. "Ha! You mean we get tuh dig outa here with you watchin'. That'll be the day!" Sneering he gave the guard his three-fingered nose salute.

"Hell no, you ninny," Hack growled. "You birds is gonna dig a gateway into that hill, then you're gonna dig out a whole damn new yard over the next year, and I'm gonna be right here to see that you do it, every rock-smashing inch of it!"

Then he called attention to the guard tower where the east and south walls joined. "Just 'cause that tower ain't manned, don't go getting no ideas. The Super figured it'd be too dangerous having a guard up there while they was blasting holes, but remember, I'll be standing right here among you with this." Hack tapped the 44–40 rifle cradled in his left arm.

Powers looked up at the square guard structure in question. Its four sidewalls were boarded almost waist-high, then opened as far as the pyramidal roof, permitting the guards an unobstructed view in all directions. The hill on the south side of the prison formed an eighteen-foot-high wall where the yard had been dug into the solid caliche. On the east side, the hill sloped downward, necessitating the long wall to extend the entire length of the prison, northward from the hill where they were working.

"Pick up those tools and start pounding," Hack cried. He moved back a few paces so that he could better watch them all, not wanting to be too near the swinging sledges.

Being smaller than the others, Powers held the drill for the huge Print who swung the ten-pound sledge with effortless regularity. The other men shoveled away loose rock shattered by the earlier blasting.

Heat and sweat irked the toiling prisoners, while the sound of ringing steel splintering rocks and the grating of shovels dragging stone chips mingled with the heavy dust shrouding the area.

And the morning ticked slowly away. The sun was a fiery orb hanging directly overhead when the whistle blew to signal the noon meal.

"You men can lay down your tools now and line up," Hack told them, his rifle cradled in the crook of his arm. "You'll have a chance to fill your bellies with beans."

Powers wiped a hand across the thin film of moisture on his upper lip. Hell, he hardly sweated anymore. Dwyer, he recalled, hadn't sweated much either, only when he had been seized with those body-shaking fits that often beset him. Otherwise, Fish hadn't been perspired, hadn't even enough meat on his rack of bones to perspire.

Lined up, the prisoners were ready to eat. At the guard's command, Powers stepped off, following in the footsteps of the other convicts. Damned Arizona sun, he thought, hot enough to bake the balls off a man without any juices. He grumbled to himself all the way up to the mess hall area where he got into line with the other prisoners without comment.

But not even the time they spent in the hot, steamy hall did much for him because he had somehow lost his appetite in the noisy, clattering area permeated with a boiled cabbage odor. He did, however, drink two glasses of cool water while picking desultorily at the food on his plate. He was glad when the whistle signaled them back to the job.

At the lineup, Hack ordered Print and Laustina to pick up a ladder from the carpenter shop building just north of the mess hall, then they marched back to the work site in silence.

"Set that ladder against the wall next to that guard tower," Hack ordered, waving the 44–40 rifle clutched in his rough fists. "And don't try anything funny, Jake, not unless you figure you can beat a bullet over that wall."

Using his impaired hand, Laustina held two fingers and thumb to his nose in the age old gesture of disrespect, but Hack merely laughed, not letting it bother him.

After placing the ladder, the men resumed their toil with sledges and shovels, gouging deeply into the caliche hill. A faint east wind wafted a slight odor of stagnant water from Gila Slough, which mingled with the musky smell of the swine yard down beyond the cemetery. And the hot, tiresome afternoon dragged on.

Under Superintendent Tarbow's policy, lifers worked until sunset, and although Powers had a shorter sentence, he was included because of his misfortune to have been in the crew with the lifers on this day. Maybe, he thought, it was because he had been with them during their escape attempt. And it had not been of his own choosing, for never would he wittingly go with such callous and brutal killers.

The sun had almost lowered to the west wall when Hack decided that the proposed cell had reached the dimensions for jail cells. The guard called to him: "Powers, you shinny up that ladder. This cell is about ready for a ventilator hole. You gotta punch a hole through about two feet of rock roof. Do a good job up there and maybe I'll see you get an easier work detail later."

Powers put down his shovel, casting an eye to the top of the cavelike cell they had carved into the hill. He moved over to the ladder and began a slow climb. Near the top of the wall, he looked over the side of the empty tower banister, noting the small chinks of rocks hurled there by the blast explosions from the preceding day. He walked along the edge away from the ladder until he stood above the cell they were working on.

"Heads up, Powers! I'm having your tools tossed up," Hack called.

Powers stood aside while Print, swinging the sledge side-armed, heaved it up to him. Seconds later, two chisels clanged on the sunbaked caliche near his feet.

"Take four paces back from this edge, then start hammering," Hack called to him. "And get a move on so we can finish before dark."

Powers held the shorter chisel in his left hand and began hammering with the other, rotating the steel drill between strokes of the hammer. Although the sun was still hot he felt better here where a listless breeze was moving up from the river below, nor was it so oppressive from dust. Exposed to the elements for centuries longer, the gray caliche crust disintegrated easily under his hammer blows until the drill dug in half its length. From then on the pounding became work again, harder and harder as the drill slowly ate its way down into the rock.

Like a swooping bird, a singular shadow caught the corner of his eye, and magiclike, he swiveled his head toward the guard tower, his hammer missing the stroke, striking the cementlike rock. He stared at the empty tower now framed in the stark light of the lowering sun.

Queer, he thought, and an odd felling crept over him. He looked hard at the ominous tower, but nothing moved, save swirls of dust occasionally floating upward from the work below. He began his hammering again, striking the drill harder in his anxiety to complete the job. Yet an eerie feeling lurked in his mind and the hint of unseen eyes prickled his skin. But never when he looked at the tower could he see anything. An unexplained fear pervaded his reason.

Mouth dry, he gritted his teeth, hammering the longer drill stem faster and faster, knowing that it was almost through the domed ceiling beneath.

He struck a blow, and in his haste still another, then the steel tool broke through the rock roof, and sailing from his hand, fell into the cell below him.

"All right, Powers," Hack called up at him. "Throw your tools down, you can finish up in the morning. Let's go eat."

Relieved, Powers tossed the hammer over the side after he had thrown the drill. He stood a moment looking westward where the dying sun had dropped below the wall. A haze was beginning to form across Yuma, and he could faintly hear cantina music as Rincon Alley inhabitants were slowly coming to life.

His glance pulled back at the tower where forty steps separated him from the ladder leaning against the wall at its base. He lingered another moment, looking eastward across the swine yard, down toward the Gila Slough. A quiet was settling over the haze of the desert.

"Dammit, Powers, you coming down or do I have to fetch you?" Hack yelled angrily, his patience worn thin after the long hot day.

"Coming," Powers answered. Fascinated, he walked trancelike toward the tower, a strange sensation raising the hackles along his spine like a cold wind blowing over his sweaty back. Staring his eyes swept the tower again, seeing nothing, hearing nothing, but neither did he care to stop and peer inside the enclosed railings.

He quickly put a foot on the top rung and took a hesitant step downward. Abruptly, a presentiment like a finger of ice touched his spine but he dared not stop now. He took another step hastily down before he heard the strange swish sounding over his head, then something cold touched his neck.

Horror strickened, he reached with both hands, groping, tearing at the thing cutting into his throat. Losing his balance, his legs kicked out and suddenly the ladder began to slide sideways along the wall as though propelled by some strange force. His scream was cut short and his struggling feet tried to walk on air when the ladder crashed to the ground. The crimson burst in his eyes before he was enveloped in the black void.

Speechless, the three convicts and Hack stared up at Powers suspended halfway up the eighteen-foot wall, quivering, but with no visible support.

And it was full minute before Hack stirred to action.

Alerted by the frantic guard who had just interrupted his evening meal, Warden Tarbow ordered the hysterical Hack to silence. "Quiet!" he snapped. "Now slow down a minute, damn it. I can't make out a thing you're saying."

He ushered the man away from the door and off the porch, not wanting to disturb his wife still seated at the table. Then he tried again. "Now tell me what happened."

Calmer now in the presence of his superior, Hack said: "I really don't know, sir. Powers had just finished punching a ventilator hole through the roof of that new cell, and he was coming down the ladder, which was leaning against the wall in the corner by the guard tower. I didn't pay him too much mind once he started down the ladder 'cause I didn't trust that three-fingered bastid or that big nigger as long as they had sledges in their hands. Not after what they done to poor old Sheaves."

Tarbow nodded. "Easy now, you're doing fine. Then what happened?"

Lamplight shining from the superintendent's doorway caught the angle of the agitated guard's jaw. He swallowed grimly, then continued: "Next thing I knew the ladder slid from under him, only he didn't fall. The ladder hit the ground but Powers just kept hanging up there in midair, kicking like a man on the gallows...only we can't see no rope!"

Tarbow took the man by the arm and started toward the sally port entrance to the prison yard. "Keep talking, Hack. Tell me the rest of it," he urged.

"Well, sir, I herded them prisoners back to their cell, then I hollered for the yard captain to bring some lanterns. I got Allison and Frettly standing by at the body now, so I came to tell you quick as I could."

After the gate guard had allowed them inside the wall, they walked rapidly through the yard to the rear wall. Tarbow saw the lanterns circling the two guards standing watch. Powers's body could be seen hanging motionless, outlined as a darkened shadow on the wall by lantern light. Closer now, he could see the dark line of blood forming a black band around the dead man's neck, the skin bulging and cut, the front of his throat having disgorged his life's blood over his drenched clothing.

"Put up the ladder," Tarbow directed the two guards. "Hold it while I go up there and take a look."

He picked up one of the lanterns and carefully climbed the ladder now positioned beside the still body. By the yellow light, he could see the man's swollen neck, then he raised his eyes upward, following the silvery sheen of the thin steel wire to where it was wrapped around a corner post of the tower. Strong, but hair thin, the steel wire was invisible from the ground.

The superintendent whistled through tense lips. "Garroted and hung in the same breath. The poor beggar's hanging by his neck bone alone," he said to the guards eagerly looking up at him. "Get another ladder alongside him, and bring a pair of cutting pliers. He's hanging by a wire."

Jittery, Tarbow came carefully down the ladder, glad to be away from the dead man. "When you get him down, take the body around to the carpenter shop. Put him on one of the workbenches. Lock the door and put a guard on it until the doctor gets here."

The superintendent started unsteadily away from the scene, then stopped. "You men keep your mouths shut until we find out what happened. I don't want the prisoners to get panicky, understand?"

Dr. Rufus Botts accepted a cigar from the box Joshua Tarbow held out for him. He stuck the end in his mouth, waving a hand to refuse the superintendent's match. "Damnation, Josh, I never seen anything like it. Evidently someone hid behind that solid banister with a wire tied to the corner post. When this Dalton Powers started down the wire, he slipped the wire noose over his head, then shoved the ladder, or maybe Powers kicked it away in his frenzy to get the garrote loose," Botts said, gesturing with his hands. "That dang wire cut clean through his neck to the bone during his struggling. Without an autopsy, I don't know if he was strangled or died of a severed jugular vein."

Tarbow shook his head as though trying to clear it, then mashed a hand across his lined face. He was tired. "Three dead prisoners within the week, two of them dying under damn strange circumstances," he muttered.

Botts rolled the cigar to the other side of his mouth with his tongue. "You think this may be part of a plot—something premeditated?" he asked.

Tired-eyed, the superintendent glanced up, his face a blank. "Frankly, I don't know what to think, Rufus."

He got to his feet and paced the length of the office, then he paused to strike a match to another lamp setting against the back wall, striving for assurance with the additional light.

"This just couldn't have been done by someone from the inside, and I sure as hell don't believe Powers did it to himself. Hack told me that Powers had walked over to the ladder and then started down. The light wasn't too good anymore, but then Hack said he was too busy keeping an eye on them lifers to pay much attention to Powers."

"The other three men out there were lifers?" Botts asked, trying to help shed some light on what had transpired.

"Yes. They were the men who killed Sheaves when he wasn't looking," Tarbow said. "And Powers was along with them when they escaped."

"Well, if the four of them escaped together, then maybe someone from the outside killed them," Botts offered. "You know a guard with a grudge could get up there without any trouble."

Things were beginning to come back into focus. Tarbow looked bleakly at the open office door. "You may be right, because that east wall butts into the hill, and then the hill becomes the south wall," he said. He remembered that when they had built this prison, the guard towers covered the area adequately. No one had taken into consideration that a blind spot was created when the one tower was taken out of operation. But then neither had he considered this when he ordered the post vacated during construction.

He squared his shoulders, setting his mind harder to the task. "A guard up there wouldn't be out of place if someone noticed him. Or if someone else came over that hill on his stomach, he just might make it to the tower without being seen, especially with the rough rocks casting long shadows when the sun dropped down below the west wall."

"But Powers climbed up the ladder right next to that tower earlier when it was still broad daylight," Butts reminded him.

"True, but maybe Powers didn't look over the banister, or maybe there was no one there yet," Tarbow said. "Hell, maybe the man didn't come up until it was almost dark."

Skeptical, Botts shook his head. "Why go to all that bother getting into the prison grounds when a man with a rifle could pick off Powers easily from the outside."

Tarbow snorted. "From where? A shot would have alerted all the tower guards. Remember, that Lowell Battery is right in line with the empty tower, and you know what a Gatling could do to the sniper."

He watched Rufus Botts's unconvinced face, then he shook a finger at the doctor. "Besides, any spot along Penitentiary Avenue is far too low to draw a bead on a man over by the southeast tower, and the cemetery and swine yards aren't much better places," he argued. "It just had to be someone who came into the prison from the south side of the hill. We don't patrol outside the walls because who the hell wants to break *into* prison?"

Botts nodded in agreement. "You're probably right, both sides are far too low. So now we come again to the question—why?"

"Why indeed," Tarbow snapped. "Good Lord, here we've got two hundred and sixty men in here all anxious to get out of here, and some jasper out there breaks in here, mind you!"

Botts's eyes followed Tarbow when he walked behind his desk and sat down with a deep sigh. He'd never seen the superintendent so disturbed before. He'd do what he could to ease the problem.

"Anyway, Josh, there's no connection between Dwyer and Powers, except they just happened to be cell mates for two days. Dwyer was a weed smoker and a drug addict, while Powers was just a nervous sneak thief. Otherwise, they never had anything in common, nor did they even bother anyone," Botts said, knowing he'd better end this conversation before Tarbow got too worked up. He pulled a fobbed watch from the small pocket below his belt, glanced at the time, then returned the watch. He waggled a finger at the desk. "Josh, I really must be on my way and the hour is getting late. For the record, these papers I signed, certify that Dalton Powers met his death at the hands of a person or persons unknown."

Tarbow arose, then reached out and shook his friend's hand. "Thank you, Rufus. You've been a big help during this sticky business."

Superintendent Tarbow sat down and drew a deep breath after Botts had departed. Now that he had a better idea of what he was up against, knowing that it could hardly be coincidental, he would take other precautions for security. He would explore all possibilities to prevent recurrence. A hard core of worry still dug into his vitals. He must keep his guards alert until this thing was out in the open, until he could understand the reasons behind whatever was going on. But at the same time he would watch each of his guards closely in case there was a killer among them. He'd keep the pressure on the guards and the prisoners as well.

He lit a cigar and settled back in his chair comfortably. He'd have to think this thing through carefully, stop what was happening around here before the prisoners became panicky, or them politicians in Phoenix got antsy enough to howl for his job. And he sure wanted to keep on being the superintendent of this prison.

Chapter Eight

"*Madre de Dios*!" Carugna pulled off his hat, then crossed himself with fervor. His startled eyes remained glued to the limp body of Dalton Powers swaying idly in midair, his gray-and-black-striped clothing, now blood soaked, was draped like a wet potato sack on his still form. The three awestruck convicts backed away, mouths agape.

So unexpected was the sight that when Hack looked up, he, too, froze. Seeing the convicts back away, he recognized the danger of the moment and knew that he must act at once before they panicked.

"Let's go, men, back to your cell!" he cried. "On the double!"

Using his rifle to jab at them, he hurried the unprotesting men at a trot back to their cell block. Glad to be away from the gruesome spectacle, they shuffled into their cell and stood speechless while they watched Hack slam the bar across the door hasp and snap the padlock.

The shock of Powers's death hovered over them like a shroud long after Hack ran back to the scene at the wall. They heard his cry to the guard, then heard it relayed again to the main tower where it became a chant: "Captain to the yard, on the double! Captain to the yard, on the double!"

The sound of running boots reached their ears and guards poured through the front gate, emptying the barracks next to the superintendent's office. Rifles at a port, they hurried in answer to Hack's call.

The spell broken, Print swung his perspiring body onto his bunk. "Ah jest can't understand what happened. One minute thet little monkey was comin' down the ladder, an' the next thing he hangin' by his neck, kickin' his feet with his throat cut."

"*Madre de Dios*," Carugna muttered again, his eyes glazed in a state of shock, sweat running down his forehead from his matted hair.

"You damn yellow greaser, stop thet mumble-jumble," Laustina snarled viciously. "Stop it, you hear!"

"We will all die," the Mexican groaned. "It is God's curse on us."

Laustina slapped the back of his knuckles across the smaller man's face. "Shut yore damn mouth, I tell you, or I'll shut it for you!"

The Mexican reeled against the iron bunks, momentarily clinging to the upright for support, while blood from his lips dribbled down his chin as he stood with head bowed.

"*Madre de Dios*," he said again weakly, staring numbly at the floor.

Eyes ablaze, lips pinched starkly in anger, Laustina took a step toward Carugna, but Print stepped between them, his hand raised to deter the three-fingered convict while he looked at the stupefied Mexican.

"Wait!" Print snapped. "Ah wanna talk to him!"

"*Madre de Dios*," Carugna moaned again, wagging his head inanely. "God has cursed us."

His eyes rolled back and forth as a vision returned from his past. As a small boy who had lived in a mission village, young Alexio had heard the story of the crucifixion from a priest. And the padre's vivid description of Christ's terrible suffering had so unnerved the lad that the story had stayed with him long after he had ventured deep into a life of sin.

Once, when he had been badly wounded after a bank robbery, he came upon a small church in a deserted village. Staggering from his horse he had crept inside before fainting from the excruciating pain. Feverish, he had awakened to see the stark morning sunlight beaming through a ragged hole in the roof. The bright rays, cast on the back wall, seemed to frame a wooden figure of Christ from which the cross had long since crumbled, and in his distraught brain, fear imprinted this image hanging on the wall, minus a cross.

Later, when he had recovered sufficient strength to ride away, the sun's rays on the damaged icon remained hidden in the subconscious recesses of his mind.

"What's this God's curse you talkin' about?" Print asked, catching Carugna by the hair and raising his face up so he could look at him.

Carugna lifted wide eyes to Print. "I see His sign on the wall," he moaned. "We will all die."

"What's this sign you bin handin' us." Print rolled his eyes over at Laustina, warning him to silence. "Ah ain't seed no such sign."

"He hung on the wall held only by the Hand of God," the terrified Mexican whispered hoarsely. "Like Christ himself."

"Shee-it!" Laustina was no longer able to contain himself in spite of Print's warning. "I don't want tuh hear no more about it! Thet damn midget jest got tangled up in some guy wires bracin' thet tower!"

"You think so?" Print asked, a deep frown furrowing his brow. "Then why we didn't see no wire when we first put the ladder agin thet tower wall?"

"How the hell would I know," the burly man cried. "You act like someone maybe hung him on purpose!"

"The Curse of God," Carugna said again, his face twitching. "First Dwyer, now this man Powers, we will all die!"

"Why, man?" Print asked. "Why do you think thet?"

"For killing those two women, cutting them like you did!" Carugna blurted out. "Now it is God's will that we die."

"Shee-it," Laustina snorted, stabbing a thumb at his chest. "You think they is the only women I ever cut or killed? An' I ain't dead yet."

It was fuzzy, but Print could understand some of what the Mexican was saying for he was only two generations out of the West Indies—where witchcraft and voodoo prevailed, and spells could be cast on one's enemies. Carugna's God—a God he was not very familiar with— could have been angered.

"Think this is you God's doin'?" he asked, and when Carugna didn't answer, he looked at the other convict.

"Shee-it," Laustina growled again. "He ain't got no God, an' if he did, do you think this God would be meddlin' around avengin' some Injun whores?"

"Those women were no whores," the Mexican whined. "They was wives of them two Quechan trackers."

"You mean them Injun bastids what found us?" Laustina cried angrily. "I'm glad their women is dead, an' I don't wanna hear no more about it!"

But the big Negro wasn't at all satisfied, perspiration hung on the flat sides of his jaws. "Maybe they's somethin' to what he say," Print said. "Them two daid men was along when we lit out."

"But, dammit, they didn't do nothin'," the burly man sneered, waggling a thick finger at Carugna for emphasis. "Remember, we was the ones who cut them squaws, an' we was the ones who rode them. Hell, even Alexio got blood on his belly dinkin' them, too, but neither of them dead men touched them squaws. An' by damn, ain't nothin' happened to none of us!"

Print mulled this over in his mind; spells usually didn't work this way. Maybe Laustina was right, maybe it was foolish to worry about the things Carguna inferred. Hell, not even the superintendent nor any of the guards seemed very disturbed at what had happened to the little shit.

Wordlessly, he climbed to the top bunk and lay with eyes wide open long after the fretful Carugna and Laustina began to snore. He strained his ears to catch the sound of boot steps moving with the lantern light around the other side of the mess hall. Evidently Superintendent Tarbow had finished examining Powers's body and was now having the the guards move him. The prison cell doors faced east and west, but by the position of the lantern lights shining down the corridor, the guards had halted at one of the shops near the main gate.

After a time the lanterns, too, faded away and Print heard no more movement. He stared up at the faintly visible high-domed ceiling, trying to recall the past. First it had been Fish Dwyer with his face blown away, then Dalton Powers mysteriously hung by a wire too thin to be seen from below.

What was it Carugna had said about the two Quechan women—that they weren't whores? By Quechan standards these women were wives, same as any white man's, but he had heard that their wedding ceremonies sure as hell were different. All it took for a Quechan to get married was for the man to spend four nights alongside a woman without touching her, then she had to prepare a meal for his family, and that was it—they were then considered hitched.

He supposed that was the way it had been with that young, firm-bodied, little wench and the Quechan tracker called Ho-Nas Good. Too bad he had cut her up so bad, but it had irked him to be tracked down by an Indian acting like a bloodhound. Not that he had any remorse over the killings, but she had been a good lay in spite of her crying in pain and terror. His thick lips spread slowly in a satisfied grin when he thought of the fight the older woman had put up while he was mounting her. Man, that had really been some-thing, just like a wildcat. Hell, she had fought fiercely all the way, and that had made it all the more enjoyable for him.

But when she had spat in his face, all the pent-up anger had flared in him—that's when he had hacked off one of her huge breasts. Rolling away from her arched body, he had laughed coarsely at her high-pitched scream when the shocked pain reached her brain. With aroused delight, he had even watched Carugna glorying on her bloody body.

And then Print suddenly was aware that he was breath-ing deeply and a dryness rasped his throat. This would never do, he thought, knowing that he shouldn't go on reliving the past. He lay quietly until his breathing had sub-sided and his ears picked up the faint sounds of revelry floating up from Rincon Alley, just west of the prison, sounds barely discernible above the raucous snores sound-ing from the cells off the corridor. But tonight, the sounds of joy were not for him, as his mind moved back over Carugna's warning. Somewhere in the jungle of his instincts as a hunted man, he felt a tinge of fear.

What if this God did have a hex on them? Or what if someone was trying to kill them one by one? Shouldn't that person's anger be directed first toward the men who had actually taken part in the bloody, raping orgy, and whose hands had wielded the mutilating knife? Or was killing off the two weakest members of the gang a buildup to create fear as part of the punishment to be forthcoming for the rest?

Hell, he had fought and killed many times, never fearing any man. So why start now. Maybe that was part of his trou-ble, he thought, he'd already spent too much time dwelling on Carugna's fetish—that this was a curse placed on them, instead of the work of some vengeful person.

Better he forget all this nonsense and be glad that he was still alive simply because that drunken judge had no use for Indians or their squaws. Alive, that's what he was, and by damn, that was how he was going to stay. He rolled over on the straw mattress, but sleep was slow in coming for him.

Superintendent Tarbow's eyes ranged irritably over the guards assembled in a semicircle on chairs around his desk. When the last man had entered he stood up to address them.

"Men, we've had three deaths, two of them covert deaths, very close together and without apparent motives. The shooting outside the mess hall will be easily accepted by the prison commissioners, because there was an attempted escape, but the deaths of Dwyer and Powers won't set well as there are no motives. We're not even sure that they are connected in any way, but this is something was must consider. In case these events are related, we have two possibilities to pursue. One, that some organized plan is being carried out by someone inside this prison with a grudge. Or, two, by someone from the outside, who is seeking retribution against some of our inmates," Tarbow said, holding up two fingers to illustrate his point.

He folded down one finger, then said: "Let's work from the first assumption that the problem is internal. We need to keep the pressure on the prisoners to disrupt any plans in being, to make them break. Now, here's how we'll do that: I want a maximum of guards watching the lines in the mess hall. The men will not be allowed outside their cells, excepting for meals, until further notice. During meal assemblies, guards will stand at each end of the corridors while the men are going to the hall, and they will stay in the cell area until the prisoners are safely locked in. While the men are in line, or eating, there will be no talking, and they will be strictly supervised. At the conclusion of the meal, the men will be searched at the door before they leave the hall. I don't want a single knife, fork, or spoon to be taken out, not even a toothpick! Nothing that can be used for a weapon will be permitted on them at anytime. Understand?"

He paused, his eyes sweeping intensely over the group, then he clenched a fist for emphasis. "Don't take any guff nor allow any horseplay from the prisoners anywhere. First convict who sounds off will be escorted to the snake pit for three days regardless of how minor the infraction is," he said firmly, smashing his fist into the open palm of his other hand. "I don't want to let anything start that might provoke trouble between the men."

His hard eyes raked the room, touching each guard. "And I want prompt action at all times! You are dismissed!"

Tarbow sat down behind the desk and watched the men file out. He remained seated long after the guards had departed. He was tired and much concerned over this latest death, for prison commissioners didn't take kindly to superintendents who permitted prisoners to be killed right under their noses. And he wasn't ready to give up this job just yet. By God, he would see that something was done about it!

Confined to such close quarters, the men became morose, and even the guards growled at each other. Tarbow, on the other hand, watched the drama unfold, taking note of everyone's reactions to the tension, and he was pleased. Someone or something would crack soon.

After the third day, Carugna stopped exhorting the Mother of God for mercy. He sat on a middle bunk, arms hanging down between his legs dejectedly, while his vacant eyes transfixed the concrete floor.

Now that Carugna no longer intoned his muttered pleas for mercy, the three-fingered convict had stopped cursing, but all was not tranquil, for Laustina's restlessness drove him to pacing. The nine-by-eight-foot cell had a tier of three bunks on each side; this did not leave much room for restlessness pacing in the center aisle.

Hedgemon Print had elected to use a top berth, and he spent most of their restricted time lying there staring at the ceiling, patiently biding the time when they would again be allowed yard privileges. His hooded eyes kept an annoyed stare riveted on the burly Laustina since he had started pacing the four-step pathway between the barred door and the back wall of the cell.

Print considered how remarkably the wild-eyed Laustina resembled a stalking shaggy bear. A patient man he was, but now this bear stomping back and forth was getting on his nerves. Sweat oozed through the pores of his skin and a wicked impulse surged through him to leap on Laustina and pound him into the floor.

He took a deep breath, knowing that such a move wouldn't help matters for them because the superintendent had warned that the slightest infraction would mean at least three days in the pit. That would increase the stress they were all under and conditions would become worse. He was sure that Tarbow wouldn't quit until he had flushed out the killer, if there really was one. It was evident that the superintendent meant to break someone by keeping the pressure on.

His high cheekbones moved when his jaw muscles tensed and a frustrated anger began working through him, rising in tempo while the burly man's boots shuffled the length of the cell. Print's muscles itched to move and his teeth sat on edge, but he held himself reined. He saw Carugna lift his eyes, his head swiveling like a puppet on a string, following the outlaw's pacing.

Suddenly Laustina stopped, then his hand shot out, grabbing a handful of Carugna's hair. "You dirty greaser, you're mockin' me!" he cried.

"*Madre de Dios,*" the astonished Mexican squealed. "I don' do nothing!"

"There you go again with thet *Dios* thing!" Laustina shouted, slapping the back of his hand across Carugna's face, then slashing the knuckles back over the other cheek. "Damn you, I told you to stop thet kind of mumble-jumble!"

A red fog of rage surged through Laustina and he started to belabor the Mexican with hamlike fists. Unable to defend himself, Carugna wrapped his arms around his head, crying out in fear.

Cat-quick, Print rolled off the high bunk onto Laustina's back, his strong arms encircling the surprised outlaw. His weight drove the burly outlaw's head against the steel bunk with a thud.

"You black sonovabitch," Laustina shrieked. "I'm gonna kill you, too!"

Above the grunts and curses, the sounds of running boots thudded in the corridor, but Print held fast to the bucking, squirming man, knowing that in his furor the burly man wouldn't stop after the guards arrived. Laustina raged against Print's powerful clutch. Twisting and turning, he tried to smash the big man against the iron uprights supporting the bunks, but Print's grip never loosened.

Keys rattled and the grated doors screeched open while two guards crowded in. "Let go of him, Print!" Harplee cried. "Break it up, you hear?"

"Ah cain't rightly do thet, Mister Harplee," Print growled through tight lips. "Old Jake here jest gone wild. He ain't gonna stop iffen ah let's go!"

Slobbering and cursing, Laustina kept threshing around; driving his powerful legs, he lunged Print against the bunks with a crash.

Carugna came to life, clutching at the chief guard's sleeve. "It is true, señor. This hombre tried to kill me, he is *tonto*!"

Harplee nodded at Allison, and the tall guard quickly slid a lead-weighted leather roll from his belt. With a quick blow, he caught Laustina just above the right temple and the outlaw went limp in Print's arms. Print eased the unconscious man to the floor, then stepped back from his exertion.

Carugna pointed a shaky finger down at Laustina. "He began hitting me for no reason," he cried. "He try to kill me! *Tonto bastardo!*"

Harplee's cold eyes covered the big Negro. "What's your story?"

Print shrugged, not wanting to say anything that would get him an invite into the snake pit, too. "It's like he said, suh," Print told them, nodding at the Mexican convict. "Jake started hitting him an' he wouldn't stop when ah told him to. He was tryin' to smash this man, so ah grabbed hold of him, but then he jest went plumb wild tryin' to stomp me agin them bunks."

Experienced from many years of such troubles, Harplee's gray eyes regarded both deeply. Satisfied of their truth, he brushed a hand down his beard, then nodded before he stepped over the fallen outlaw and edged his way through the doorway. He motioned another guard to enter the cell.

"Frettly, you and Allison drag Laustina down to the pit. Make sure that he's chained good before you lock the door. Maybe three days in that hole will take some of the piss and vinegar out of him."

He stood aside while the two guards, each supporting an arm and shoulder, dragged the bull-like convict from the cell. Then Harplee led the way down the corridor to unlock the gate at the south end of the cell block. The two guards followed him across the dirt yard, dragging their unconscious burden.

The snake pit was carved into the solid wall, which also served as the south wall of the prison. A short tunnel-like corridor, about eight feet long, led into the dark cell. The inside door was made of sheet-iron, with a small rectangular cutout near the bottom so that food and drink could be placed into the cell without opening the door. The outer door was made of bars. The cell was large, about fifteen by fifteen feet, with a small hole in the twenty-foot ceiling to provide some ventilation. A thin stream of light sometimes found its way down through the hole when the sun was directly overhead, otherwise the room was dark.

With the sheet-iron door open, as it now was, an iron ring set in the middle of the concrete floor could be seen. Frettly dragged a chain and two large padlocks from a back corner, and he quickly wrapped the chain end around Laustina's ankle and snapped the lock. Then, threading the other end of the chain through the ring set in the floor, he clenched the other lock.

"That oughta hold him for a spell," Frettly said. "At least he ain't gonna take no walk."

Allison chuckled. "That's for sure," he said, and when a groan was heard from the convict on the floor, he added: "Old Three-fingers is startin' to wake up. We better get out of here before we have to fight our way clear, Fred."

The two guards carefully closed the iron door and bolted it, knowing that the inside of the pit would be almost pitch black now. Slamming the outer door and snapping the lock, Frettly dusted his hands. "That, by God, is that!"

"Tuesday noon through Friday noon." Allison counted the days on his fingers. "I'll report that to the Super, so he can arrange to turn Laustina loose on Friday."

"Sure hope them three days soften him up," Frettly said dryly. "I don't care to be draggin' that heavy bastard back an' forth anymore."

"Amen," Frank Allison echoed.

Chapter Nine

Honas Good watched Sheriff Waringer wipe the back of his hand across the stubble on his chin. The sun was just creeping above the Yuma Exchange Saloon, casting a shadow over the corral fence where he and Palma stood facing the lawman.

"Evidently them two followed him into the saloon," Waringer said. "Anyway, the bartender told that two men came into the bar about eight o'clock last night. They pulled guns and held everyone at bay. They didn't bother the cash register none even though there were only five other men in the room. All they took was a saddlebag away from a gent who had come in earlier. When they left in a hurry, all the men in the saloon took off after them, following the footsteps of the man who had just been robbed."

The lawman moved away from the corral fence and pointed a gnarled finger across the empty lot. "The barman said the two robbers had horses tied to this fence. When they came out of the saloon, they forked their broncs and took off across that field down to First Street, then west out of town."

He pointed a finger at the ground. "Every damn fool in the barroom took off after them fellows, and as you can see by all these tracks, they came from every which way.

Guess they chased them robbers out beyond the town lights, but lost them in the dark of the desert," he told them. "I didn't get back to Yuma until just before midnight, so when I was told what had happened, I decided I'd get you and Palma first thing this morning so we could start out fresh. Dark as it was last night I couldn't see much use wandering around in the dark, what with all them tracks botched up by them would-be pursuers."

Honas nodded. "We can follow First Street out of town a ways, then quarter back and forth until we weed out their tracks," he said. "Then we can go to work."

Waringer nodded sagely. "Them robbers wouldn't stay on the road very long once they got away from Yuma. They wouldn't want to risk anyone seeing them."

"What happened to the man who was robbed?" Honas asked.

The lawman shook his head. "Don't know. He seems to have disappeared, which makes this kinda touchy. What appears to be an armed robbery may turn out to be nothing without a person to file a complaint. Neither barman nor any of the other customers was robbed," Waringer said dejectedly. "But, I figure we oughta scout around out there for another reason. You see, a man rode in from the Clip Mine last night shortly after I got to bed. He said that three men had robbed their paymaster of a three-thousand-dollar payroll. He couldn't give much of a description of the robbers because one of them had lamped the paymaster with the butt end of his six-shooter before they stole the saddlebags with the payroll money."

"So now you think the man who was robbed of the saddlebags in the saloon was one of them?" Honas asked. "And maybe the bags held the payroll money?"

Waringer shrugged, "Well, it might have been all three of them. Could be that some double crossing had been going on."

"But if it isn't the same saddlebag," Honas said, "then we don't really know if a robbery occurred in the saloon."

"I think that we would have probable cause," Waringer said. "The barkeeper saw a saddlebag taken at gunpoint even though no one else was bothered."

"That's probable cause, all right," Honas agreed. "They've got a pretty good headstart, so we better take out."

"And when we catch them jiggers, they can explain their little game with the saddlebags to the paymaster back at the Clip Mine. It's only about thirty miles north of here."

Palma led the three horses from the corral, holding out two sets of reins.

Waringer took his reins before he said: "I don't want any gunplay until we know for sure that those are the men we want."

Boots crunched on gravel and they turned their attention to a slim man approaching. "Yore deputy said yuh was lookin' fer me, sheriff," the man said, sunlight slanting from the angle of his thin face.

"Yeh, Hobbs," the lawman said. "I heard you rode with that bunch last night when they went chasing after them holdup men."

"Yup. When them jaspers threw down on us, we thought it was a stickup, for sure," Hobbs said, "but all they taken was them saddlebags off thet queer-lookin' gent standin' by hisself at the bar."

"Queer-looking?" Waringer asked.

"Well, his one eye didn't track jest like the other one did." The man used his hands to describe his words. "An' one ear wasn't all there. Hit was all raggety like some one'd been chewin' on hit."

"What about the chase you went on?"

"Well, soon's them two lit out," Hobbs said, "we run fer our horses an' peeled out after them. They headed 'cross Brinley, then west out on First Street. We could tell their direction by the way old man Neahr's dogs was carryin' on, but once they got away from the lights, we lost track of them."

Waringer massaged the bristles on his square chin again. "That when you boys decided to come back?"

Hobbs nodded slowly. "Well, no. Old Jake an' his boys didn't want to be wastin' valuable drinkin' time stumbling around in the dark. This jasper offered me an' Zeb ten dollars each to ride with him. Bein' almost broke, we roweled spurs with him 'bout another hour without catchin' sight nor sound of them two robbers. Zeb finally told thet jasper we had enough. We took our money an' come back."

"That fellow ever manage to say what was in them saddlebags?" the sheriff asked.

"Naw. He wasn't talkative worth a damn until it came to cussin' us fer wantin' to leave him."

Waringer smiled weakly. "Reckon he put up a fuss over payin' you."

"Yer damn right," Hobbs growled, "but Zeb offered to straighten out his other eye iffen he didn't pay up, an' yuh know how persuasive Zeb kin be!"

"The he did pay you."

"Yup. Took the money outa his shirt pocket," Hobbs told him.

"Anything more you can tell us?" Waringer asked, and when the man shook his head, he added: "Care to come along with us? I can deputize you."

But the lean cowboy wasn't the least bit interested. "Naw. I had my worthless ride last night," he told them. "Besides, with this ten-spot I got from thet jasper, it'd be a shame fer me to git very far from the Exchange. When they opens the door of this saloon at ten o'clock, I'm gonna be standin' right at the front door."

The sheriff wagged his head at the thought of ten o'clock whiskey, then he jerked his thumb at the horses before he spoke. "We won't learn any more around here, Honas, and that sun keeps getting higher by the minute."

The Quechan squinted toward the east where the yellow rays where topping the Gila Mountains. Somewhere nearby a housewife was cooking breakfast, and the smell of bacon wafted on the warm morning air. But having just eaten, he nodded in agreement, his face still inscrutable.

"Then let's go, Sheriff." He could not have said what moved him to accept this job. Maybe he needed time to think, to get away from the prison. None of the convicts there would be going anywhere; he didn't have to worry about a lapse of time before he settled his debt with the men who had killed his wife. Besides, getting at them was going to be much harder right now.

News shunted around Yuma indicated that Superintendent Tarbow had doubled his guard efforts, and he had restricted all prisoners to their cells allowing them outside only during meal times. He knew that he'd have to let things rest for the time being.

With an irritable swing of his shoulders, Honas climbed into the saddle, and when the sheriff and Palma had mounted, he sent the horse across the vacant field behind the corral. They rode down Brinley, keeping off the railroad tracks until they reached First Street, then spurring their horses into a gallop, they rode westward, leaving the outskirts of Yuma to a chorus of barking dogs lying in the early morning shade of the last house.

The road diagonaled southward through yellow flowered greasewood and stretched out toward the endless horizon. Weather-beaten cactus stemmed through the grainy soil at sparse intervals while wagon tracks and hoofprints thinned out with each passing mile. Occasionally, Palma or Honas slid from the saddle to examine horse dung, or knelt for a closer inspection of shoe prints, noting the different configurations created by wear or dents in the horseshoes.

Honas pointed at the rocky hills to the west hanging faintly above the distant haze. "If they traveled over those hills, they could pass San Luis without being seen by keeping to the river until they got to Mexico, but if they go eastward, they can also get around San Luis, only that means they would be in the desert most of the way," he said.

"You're the tracker," Waringer said. "Which way do you think we should go?"

A faint smile tugged at the corner of Honas Good's mouth. "Our way is clear. We will ride west along the river."

Waringer was surprised. "You mean with all these stray tracks, you think you can find the ones belonging to those robbers?"

The tension pulled tighter at the Indian's lips, but the smile never came through. Taut-reining his horse, he pointed to the sky at the horizon. Numerous specks were circling over a canyon stemming into the low hills.

"I think those birds have found some of your men for us," Honas said, nodding at the vultures floating in the distance.

Waringer swung his horse around and faced the hills. "I'll be damned. You're right. Well, let's get with it," he growled. "I'd like to get home in time to get some sleep tonight."

The morning drowsed on while they cantered toward the misty blue of the foothills, riding in silence. Occasionally a lizard scampered across their trail seeking a cooler place to rest. Spumes of dust hovered over their heads while they moved through the shimmering heat waves toward the hills.

While he rode, Honas kept an eye on the soaring vultures and when they finally glided down into a wash, he kicked his heels hard against the horse's flanks. The three men rode into the low cut where the greasewood flats had given way to rolling slopes and shaley cutbanks. With a

loud flutter of wings, the ominous birds struggled awkwardly to become airborne above the still body. The man
lay beside a mesquite bush, partially sheltering him from
the sun, and judging from the hole in his forehead, it was
easy to see that he was dead, even before they dismounted.

They stood looking at the body, knowing that they had
arrived just before the vultures had started their pecking in
earnest, for the man's eyes were open and still intact.

"From the description given by the Exchange bartender,
this is the same man who had come into the saloon with the
saddlebags," Waringer said. He knelt at the man's side.
"See, his eye is cocked off to the left, and this ear's half
gone."

Then he stood up, his eyes drifting among the thin
bushes. "Probably got his ear bitten off during a fight years
ago. Looks like they took his horse, too."

Honas said something in his native tongue to his father-
in-law. Palma nodded, and disappeared into the bushes.
Honas strode behind a clump of mesquite, then he crawled
slowly across the rocky soil on hands and knees scanning
the ground as he moved. After a time, he got up and came
to where the lawman stood. He held out two .30-caliber
cartridge cases.

"They knew he was following so one of them waited for
him behind those bushes," Honas said, "and he rode right
into their ambush."

"That figures," the sheriff said. "He was hit twice—once
in the chest, then again in the forehead up real close. Probably to finish him off while he lay helpless."

Honas nodded, then said: "I sent Palma back up the
ravine to see where they hid their horses while they waited
for this one to fall into their trap."

"Figure they both shot at him?"

The tracker shook his head. "No, there are tracks of only
one man waiting in the brush. The other man stayed with

the horses farther back so they wouldn't whinny and give
away the ambush."

Palma's knee-length moccasins scuffed sand when he
slid down the bank. He spoke rapidly in his native tongue,
gesturing with his hands as he spoke, and Honas inter-
preted for Waringer.

"He said this ravine takes a bend farther up, that's where
the man waited with the horses. Judging from the manure it
is not over two hours ago," he told the lawman before
pointing up the incline. "Then those men took this one's
horse before they started over the hill toward the river."

"Well then, let's start after them," Waringer said.

But the Quechan shook his head, and when the sheriff
raised quizzical eyebrows, he said: "These men don't know
we are so close. Why not ride hard on this side until this
afternoon, then cross over the hill. By then we can be in
front and wait for them to come to us."

Waringer mulled that over for a moment, thinking the
idea had merit. "It just might work, especially if we're that
close to them now, but in the meantime, let's shallow-bury
this one. We can pick him up on the way back," he said. "If
not, at least the vultures won't get him."

The two Quechans exchanged glances, not understanding
the white man's weakness in burying an enemy. "This man
was a robber, maybe worse," asked. "Why do you do this?"

"If you two won't help me, I'll do it myself," Waringer
growled. "I can't let a man lay while them vultures shred
him to pieces before the coyotes get his bones."

Knowing that the sheriff was a stubborn man who wouldn't
leave until the body was protected, the two Quechans helped
scoop out a shallow hole, then cover the body with a mound
of sand.

"If things go right, we just could be digging him back up
before long," Waringer said, mopping a red bandana across
his damp brow before settling his hat.

"Then now is the time to eat," Palma said. "Since we have stopped, a little more time taken will not matter."

Honas untied the canvas bag fastened behind his saddle. Opening the sack, he handed the sheriff a thick slice of dried meat and a small round loaf of hard bread, traditionally made by the Quechans from ground-up, dried mesquite beans. Taking similar portions from the canvas sack, the two Indians swung into the saddle. The three men ate as they rode, munching on the dry but nourishing food, washing it down with water from their canteens.

The sun was directly overhead when Honas decided their pace must be quickened. "Better we ride hard for a time," he directed, and when Waringer agreed, he kicked his heels to the horse's flanks, and they rode at a fast clip, staying as near to the low hills as the terrain permitted.

It was midafternoon, when the tracker signaled a stop. He pointed to a craggy opening in the rocks. "We can go through here and come out well above the river on the other side," he told Waringer. "Maybe we're ahead of them, but we better be careful just in case we're not. Follow me."

The trail up the rocky pass became a shaley bank too steep for the sliding horses, and they were forced to dismount and pull the horses by their bridles. Tugging and puffing, they clattered up the slope to solid ground, then in single file they followed Honas over the ridge.

While the animals rested, the young Quechan scanned the terrain, his dark eyes moving slowly back and forth until he found what he sought. Then his eyes lingered on a movement several hundred yards north of them.

"They come," he announced simply. "Palma, you keep the horses quiet, while we crawl down and intercept them. If we need help, you can cover us from here."

While the older Quechan gathered the horse's reins, Waringer, rifle in hand, followed Honas's lead, crouching and moving silently down the rocky slope. Creeping from boulder to boulder, they took advantage of every bit of cover until they were in a line to intercept the two outlaws. Halting behind a rocky outcropping, they waited quietly while their quarry rode toward them.

Still sixty yards away, the two men suddenly halted, strangely suspicious. With a cry, one of the men threw himself from the saddle, scrambling for cover behind a towering rock.

Waringer fired, the flat crack of his rifle knocking the other man from his saddle, before his frightened horse spun, raising on hind feet in panic.

"Damn it!" Waringer cursed. "Wonder what spooked them?"

Two shots cracked and chips flew from the rock they were hiding behind. Angrily, the sheriff stood up, pumping four rounds in succession in the direction of the outlaw's shots. The bandits were now hiding behind rocks separated by a narrow defile, and they fired alternately, first one, then the other would lean out to shoot.

"Damn," Waringer muttered to Honas. "Evidently I only wounded the one I hit."

Timing the alternating fire, Honas stood quickly, and drew a bead where the next man would appear, shooting when he stepped out. An answering yelp brought a grin to Waringer's face when the man spun from sight.

"By damn," he cried. "You nicked one of them that time."

Then the other outlaw, crouching low, ran from cover toward his wounded partner and Honas snapped another shot, the bullet catching the man just below the knee, stumbling him behind the protective rocks. But a loud clatter of sliding shale from behind the rocks spelled more trouble for the bandits, and a piercing scream rent the air. Another clatter of rocks signaled the outlaw's slide backward into a deep hole.

"Help me, Osmond, they's snakes down here! Aaaah!" the terrified voice pleaded. "Help me, I'm bit!"

The young Quechan drew a bead where he thought the pit was in relation to the other man behind the rock, and when the bandit stepped into the open, he fired. The bullet slammed the man against the boulders, staggering him before he fell, and his rifle clattered down the bank.

"Aaaah! Dammit, help me," the pitiful scream came again, echoing in the cavern, and Honas stood up, rifle ready, but Osmond never moved.

He motioned Waringer toward the upper side of the outlaw's shelter while he crouched and ran forward, expecting momentarily to hear the thunder of a rifle. Behind the rocky shelter, he reached the outlaw lying facedown in the shale. Turning the man over with the toe of his boot, he saw that he was dead.

"Sheriff, come on in, it's all over," he called. Then he shouted louder: "Palma, bring a rope. There's a man down here in a hole full of rattlesnakes."

The older Quechan came sliding down the bank on a run, lariat in hand, in answer to Honas's call. Waringer inspected the dead man, then walked over to the pit to look down on the man crouched fearfully at the bottom of a ten-foot hole.

"Help me, geez, they're killin' me," the outlaw pleaded, his stark eyes white against the shadows in the pit. "Help me."

Honas twirled the rope loop into the hole, circling the man's shoulders. "Slide it under your arms. We'll pull you up."

"Hurry," the man wailed, "I'm dyin'."

Honas and the sheriff began to draw the man up, hand over hand, and when the outlaw's body bumped a side rock, he screamed again: "Aaaah! One got me!"

Dragging the writhing man over the edge of the pit, they stretched him on the ground. Wounded, frightened, and full of snake venom, the bandit was reduced to slobbering babble.

"Crissake, help me," he moaned, head shaking like a dog with ague. "Help me."

Waringer held the man's shoulders while Honas drew his knife, not knowing where to start cutting first to drain poison. Raw fang wounds dribbled blood from a bump on the man's forehead at the hairline, while two more fresh puncture marks below the swollen left eye were turning a hideous blue. Twin trickles of blood flowed from a huge lump at the base of the man's right ear.

Honas's eyes met Waringer's, and he shook his head signaling hopelessness. Spittle dribbled from the corners of the man's mouth and he feebly tried to brush a hand across it. Before the swollen hand dropped away, Honas pointed to another set of puncture marks behind the bruised thumb.

Waringer nodded. Both men arose, then moved away from the paralyzed bandit. "No doubt he's got a lot more bites on his body that we can't see. God, what a way to die, but there's nothing we can do for him. If the poor bastard was a horse, I'd shoot him."

The sheriff walked back to where the robbers had left their three horses before taking cover when the shooting began. Unbuckling the saddlebag from a horse, he peered inside.

"Here's the payroll, all right," he said. Catching up the three horses' reins, he led them back to where the dead men lay. "Money's here, evidently these two, and the man we buried, robbed the Clip Mine paymaster. Maybe they had a falling out, or that other man tried to take off with the loot all by himself."

Waringer looked at the swollen body and waggled his head sympathetically. "Imagine, dying in a hole full of snakes," he said. "At least the so-called 'Snake Pit' up at our prison don't kill a man." Then he remembered something. "Speaking of snake pits, Superintendent Tarbow put that wild Three-fingered Jake Laustina in the pit for trying to kill a cell mate during a squabble at the prison."

"When?" Honas asked quickly.

"Yesterday," Waringer said. "Gave him three days to cool off. He was trying to strangle that Mex who was with him when they killed your..." He clamped his jaws shut, not wanting to open old wounds, and when the Quechan didn't answer, he quickly changed the subject and began to sum up their situation.

"Guess the man over there is Osmond, at least that's what this one called him while them snakes was gnawing on him down in the hole," he said, pointing to the outlaw Honas had shot earlier. "These two must have caught up with that other jasper in the saloon and took their saddle-bags back. After they left, he paid Hobbs and Zeb to go with him to help follow them."

Honas agreed. "When Hobbs and Zeb deserted him, he followed alone and when he caught up with them, they killed him and stole his horse," he said, then nodded his head at the fallen outlaws. "What do you intend to do with them?"

The lawman looked skyward, judging the time. "I want you and Palma to load them on their horses and pack them back to Yuma. And pick up that man we shallow-buried, 'cause I want him, too. Meanwhile, I'll run that payroll back to the mine. With any luck, I'll be back in Yuma by midnight."

Palma opened his mouth to protest, but clamped his jaws when he caught the sharp look Honas threw him. Why, he thought, did the white lawman want to bring an enemy back? Why even bother to have buried them at all? But he would abide by what his son-in-law wanted to do, thus he nodded in agreement.

"We'll do it, Sheriff," Honas said. "Then we'll drop them off at the undertaker's and tell him to hold them for you."

Waringer's eyes studied the tall Quechan, knowing his views against the showing of any consideration to an outlaw. He nodded, then shouldering the saddlebags, he picked his way up the steep slope to where Palma had earlier tethered their horses.

Honas stood looking down into the pit, watching the agitated snakes scurry back and forth, still alarmed from the unexpected scare of the outlaw falling into their midst.

He motioned to Palma to help him, and they loaded Osmond's body over the saddle, tying it tightly in place; but when the snake-bitten robber moaned incoherently, his eye swollen blue and grotesquely closed, Honas drew his six-gun, and reversing his grip to the barrel, he struck down sharply, knocking the man unconscious. He knew that the man would be dead from venom before he woke up from the force of the blow. They draped the stunned body over the saddle and fastened it tightly.

Then Honas did a strange thing. He emptied the contents of the canvas food sack on the ground, then he took a thin leather thong from around his waist and formed a noose at one end. Searching among the bushes until he found two long branches that suited him, he cut them off. Then he trimmed them, leaving a fork at the end of each stick.

Handing a pole to Palma, he explained his plan quickly, using their native tongue. Laying on his stomach at the edge of the pit with a forked stick in one hand and the looped thong in the other, he told Palma to lie with his stick beside him. Then the older Quechan began jiggling his stick, catching a snake's attention, while Honas moved his pole into striking distance.

Cat-quick, Honas's stick forked the snake's head, pinning it to the sandy pit bottom. Keeping the snake pinned with one hand, he dangled the thong carefully until the noose slipped over the rattler's head. Slowly, he pulled it taut, then he dragged the writhing, fighting snake up the side of the pit.

Palma held the canvas sack open while Honas guided the tail into the bag, then lowered the snake. The older Indian quickly set the sack on the ground, pinning it with his stick. Honas jiggled the thong back and forth in the bag opening until the snake managed to squirm free of the noose, then he jerked the thong from the sack.

Selecting only the smaller snakes in the pit, they were able to pull up three more from the agitated, squirming mass, then gingerly they transferred them to the bag. Honas tied the sack shut, then bound it to the end of Palma's stick. With his knife, he cut the stick down to a three-foot length before he stopped to wipe the perspiration from his brow.

Observing his actions, his father-in-law laughed raucously at his discomfort until Honas responded with a tight grin. Then Palma took the end of the stick and carried the bag of snakes to Osmond's horse, where he tied the deadly cargo to the saddle horn on the nervous animal. Snakes in a sack wouldn't have room to strike, he thought, but even if they did, the outlaw Osmond was beyond caring.

"We better hurry," Honas said. "Catching these snakes has moved the sun more than an hour. We must pick up the other dead man like the sheriff asked us."

The older Quechan nodded. "Never fear, we will be in Yuma by dark," he said, squinting up at the sun standing above the hills on the Mexican side of the Colorado River.

"Then we must hurry." Honas's face had tightened, his eyes were again cold. "You will take the dead men to the coffin maker while I hide the snakes in the old burial ground below the smelter, to wait until the prison sleeps."

"It is good, my son," Palma said, "and I know that you will do what is necessary."

Honas was touched, for seldom did his father-in-law show affection as he did today. "Yes, my father," he said evenly, his dark eyes touching the older man's seamy face, for Palma, too, had sorrowed deeply over the loss of his wife and daughter. "I will see that these snakes bite again before the moon sets this day."

And Palma nodded his head, knowing that his son-in-law always spoke the truth.

Chapter Ten

On the last day of his life, Three-fingered Jake Laustina greeted the dawn with a curse. He lay on the cool concrete floor trying to gather his wits for his head ached and his throat was rasped dry. The wild surge of anger that had seized him two days earlier had subsided to a smoldering hatred toward his Mexican cell mate, Carugna. The lump above his right temple where Frank Allison had struck him with the leathered weight still throbbed, and the pulsing made it difficult to focus on past events. When he had awakened to find himself in this darkened cell remembrance brought the red fog of anger suddenly sweeping over him, causing him to shout and curse at the top of his lungs again. Ranting and raving, he had spent the first day raging violently until he had collapsed, sweating and sobbing in a pitiful heap.

Faintly, he recalled the reason that he was in this damned cell, remembering how he had smashed his fists against Carugna's face before the unexpected strength of Print's huge arms had encircled his chest, squeezing him like giant pincers. He didn't realize that Print was that strong, and it was something he would remember when they met again. He would never again let that bastard get an advantage on him. By damn, he had a score to settle up with both of them, the stinking Mex and that big black bastard.

Memory eased his anger momentarily when he thought of the encounter. Hell, he would have battered himself free if them guards hadn't come when they did. By damn, he had been pounding Print into them iron bunks hard, hurting him, until that damn Allison caught him on the temple with that lead-weighted roll. And now, by damn, that was another score he would settle one day. Christ, how he hated Frank Allison, and all the other guards for that matter; anger became a sour bile rising in his throat, prodding him to action.

He rose to his knees, and pounding both fists down on the concrete floor, felt the thud ripple upward along the muscles of his arms until it reached the pulsing in his temples. Then he yelled deeply, cursing aloud until the caliche walls rang with the rasping hoarseness in his throat. But after a time he was forced to stop when the futility of the act sobered him.

Resting on his knees, he thought how he had ranted and raged at the top of his voice during the last two days, cursing the guards and his cell mates as well. A thin shaft of pale light drew his attention and he looked up at the round ventilator hole in the high ceiling. This cell never became light and it was only when the sun was directly overhead that any rays were able to filter down for a few minutes before the cell again returned to darkness.

He suddenly realized that it was noon again, starting the third day, and if he behaved, he would be freed at noon tomorrow. Rubbing a hand over his two-day stubble of beard, a calm, relaxed feeling swept over him. Better behave he thought. He had had his fill of solitary confinement and he wanted to get out of here. And all he had to do was sit quietly for the rest of this day and he would be out in time for the noon meal tomorrow.

He sat back and straightened his legs to ease the shackles fastened to the large iron ring embedded in the floor.

Damn, this place smelled, he groused, no toilet facilities, not even a bucket. Hell, when a man had to go, he just used a corner of the cell with nothing to cover it up. No wonder the heavy odor seemed to be a permanent part of the cell.

Well, he wouldn't be in here much longer, not old Three-fingered Jake, by damn. He'd be patient and wait out the rest of the day in silence. Yelling didn't help, 'cause nobody could hear any sounds from here, and even if they did, they wouldn't pay no mind. And with this decision, a great weight seemed to lift from him, and being mentally and physically tired, he dozed fitfully.

At noon, the rattle of the small metal flap in the door signaled that bread and water containers were being pushed through the slot into the cell. After eating the small loaf of bread and washing it down with the tin cup of water, he stretched out and slept soundly for the first time in two days.

How little or how long he had been asleep, he didn't know, nor did he know what had awakened him. The long deep breath he drew was filled with the odor of human waste from the corner where he had last defecated. When he moved his hand along the chain that secured him to the ring in the floor, he felt a strange sensation, a sensation of fine dirt falling from above on his bare arm.

Looking upward, he tried to see the ventilator hole in the high ceiling, but the darkness prevailed. He drew back when a scratching noise came from the ceiling and more dirt cascaded downward. Someone was up there, and he caught his breath. Instinctively he crawled backward from the floor ring as far as his leg chains would permit. He lay quietly on his side, listening intently.

An involuntary gasp slipped from his lips when a soft plop sounded on the floor, then three more sounds followed in quick succession when other objects hit the floor. The gloom suddenly seemed to curdle in his face; a chilling darkness hung around him like a shroud. Then a slither sounded, and although he could not see in the darkness, his eyes followed the faint swish moving across the floor.

Strange things were in the cell with him, and his body tensed. Cold sweat oozed from the pores of his skin, and he tried to see shapes in the darkness, conjuring movements where none were visible

Jaws clamped, he heard a creeping stealth near his feet and he caught his breath sharply, for this time there was no doubt in his mind what was in the black cell with him. A buzzing whir goose-pimpled his flesh when the writhing stopped, and he froze, horrified.

Good Christ, a rattlesnake! Terror parched his throat while his eyes focused toward his feet, trying to penetrate the Stygian blackness. His straining ears heard the whisper of another slithering sound near his head before the angry rattle sounded. Every nerve in his body twisted and jerked, his wildly dilated eyes stabbed desperately at the darkness.

Two more buzzings sounded near the iron ring in the floor, signaling more snakes, and blind panic coursed through his veins.

"Halp! They's snakes in here!" he cried out in terror, knowing that no one would hear him or even care if they did. Throat sandy and parched, he pinched his lips, cutting off the scream building in his chest, and he gained control of himself with rising anger that recognized this for what it was: someone was trying to kill him!

Hell, it had to be one of the guards. Didn't they all hate him? Hadn't he lost two of his fingers because Homer Sheaves had smashed them with his rifle butt the last time he had been in this cell, smashed fingers that were later amputated because gangrene had set in.

Then he remembered that Sheaves was dead, remembered how he had crushed the hated guard's head with the rifle butt while he lay stunned after Print had struck him with the heavy adobe block. His mind spun, seeking to pin a name on who might have dropped these snakes down the ventilator hole. Was it Allison? Frettly?

Somehow they didn't fit the deed. Was it Carugna's God, or even worse, one of those damn Indians? Maybe that was it, maybe the Indians were behind these deaths.

He listened again but heard no further sound from the snakes. If he didn't panic, if he lay perfectly still, the snakes might not bite him, he thought, striving to get his mind functioning. But how long could he lay motionless? The answer came ironically back to him—all night, by damn, if he had to! Then he cursed the thought away.

Yet he lay there frantically waiting, but nothing further happened. All too vivid in his mind was the desperate knowledge that he must remain motionless, and he could not allow himself to be stampeded—he dared not! Then the roundabout blackness turned rigid, and the only sound was his own slow, hesitant breathing.

Sweat oozed from his face while he lay on his side, his right arm half under his body, where it had been when he was first surprised by the snakes. A cold loneliness closed over him when the tired feeling struck his neck. Unfortunately, when he had heard the rattles, he had raised his head in turning, and now he lay holding his head erect, too frightened to move. Not accustomed to such a position, cramps were developing along the muscles of his neck.

He let out a slow breath and scowled bitterly for a numbness was starting in the arm pinned under his heavy body. With the blood supply restricted, a tingle like the pricking of tiny needles began in his fingertips, then moved slowly up his arm. Damn! Why did he have to lie like this!

It was torture to have his arm throttled so, and every cringing muscle in his aching shoulder and neck longed to relieve the pressure of his tense body. When the shock of his initial fright had worn off, he knew that he must take a chance and move his arm while he still had some control over it.

Straining his ears for sound, he heard nothing. Maybe the snakes had crawled far enough away so that he could move his arm, maybe ease the numbing cramp in his neck. Teeth clamped against his lower lip, he gingerly lowered his head to the floor, feeling relief from the dull neck pain at once.

So far, so good, he thought, his mind still wrestling with the frightful paralysis of fear. He tensed his muscles, then slowly arched his back upward a scant distance before he tried to slide his arm from under his body, but the strength had fled when his arm had turned numb. Gradually he inched his left hand across his stomach until it touched his numbed hand, a hand that felt cold and lifeless. Sweat, exuded by fear, hung heavy on his face as he began to pull the numbed arm free from the weight of his body.

And then Three-fingered Jake Laustina's luck ran out— for a chain link clinked at his ankle, and sounding deafeningly loud in the tense silence, he spasmodically jerked his foot. Lightning fast, an aroused snake struck, sinking fangs deep into his exposed shinbone. Pained he cried out hoarsely in surprise, kicking with both feet, and the whirring of the rattles droned around him when he tried to sit up. He screamed in pain and horror when a second snake nailed his outflung hand, but he managed to grab the reptile's head with his other hand and he hurled it against the far wall. Just then another bite forked his leg and he called out in defiance before jumping to his feet as his wild frenzy turned to unholy anger, and he began to rattle his tether chain back and forth.

"Come and get it, you slimy bastards!" he cried. "Let's see you bite me now!"

He reached down and grasped a snake that was wrapping itself around his leg, and when it punctured his hand, his obsessive rage swept over him and he gripped its head and ripped it from the squirming body with his other hand.

Then using the headless snake like a whip, he lashed out right and left at the floor.

"Crawl, damn you, crawl!" he shrieked, running in a wide circle, flailing with the snake as he ran, the chain twisting while he moved. "Where are you now, damn you!"

Then with a surge of inhuman strength fueled by insane fury, he jerked at the twisted chain—it cut deeply into his leg before it broke, and he stumbled heavily against the far wall before he regained his balance. When his benumbed mind realized that he was free, he ran around in the black of the cell using the chain now as a flail.

"I'll kill you apple eatin' sonovabitches!" he shrieked as he ran, swinging the broken chain, sparks chipping from the concrete floor. "Haaa-eee! You slimy bitches, I'm comin' after you now!" he cried, gasping for breath. "Where are you, I don't hear you rattlin' none. Now who's afraid!"

His madness left him with a spurt of muscular contraction for a moment, then sweating profusely, with his huge chest heaving in throaty rales, spittle drooling from his peeled lips, he looked upward at the black of the high ceiling sensing that someone was up there.

Gasping for air like a spent horse, he raged in the darkness: "You shit-eatin' bastard up there, if you got any guts, come down an' face me, you hear!"

Sobbing, frustration clamped the set of his jaws and he turned numbly before his brain failed—his lungs were a huge bellows gasping for air against the tightened bands of his chest. And when his great heart gave out, Jake Laustina crashed headlong into the sheet-iron door in a swollen heap.

There was no further sound heard through the ventilator hole from the dark cell below, and Honas Good folded up his canvas sack into a small roll and tucked it into his belt. Then he took the short stick that had been tied to the sack for safety while carrying the snakes, and with a looping sweep of his arm, heaved it toward the southwest guard tower.

Waiting until he heard the stick clatter off the wall, he rose to a crouch and ran swiftly and quietly down the caliche hill from whence he came. Behind him he heard the guard shouting an alarm, knowing that soon many men with lanterns would be swarming the prison yard.

He trotted westward along Prison Lane toward Yuma, his footsteps soundless in the ankle-deep dust. Then he angled toward First Street, moving quickly to avoid the lights from the Colorado Hotel until he reached Rincon Alley. Minutes later, he pushed open the door to French Frankie Coneaut's back room, and entered the murky interior.

Palma raised his glass of brandy in salute when Honas nodded in answer to the unspoken question on his face.

Coneaut poured a glass of liquor and handed it to the young Quechan. A look of interest was on Coneaut's face. "Palma tells me you have returned tonight from bringing in the bodies of the men who rob the big mine payroll," he said.

"Yes," Honas acknowledged, his face inscrutable. A half smile tugged at his taut lips when a thought struck him. "And you will no doubt remember to tell the sheriff, if he should ask, that we have been here with you all night."

"Ho, ho," Coneaut cried, a devilish gleam in his obsidian eyes. "By God, now these are times for shrewdness an' stealth, my friends."

He poured another round of drinks, then raised his glass in salute. "Of course you were both here all night, an' we have empty bottles to prove it, no?" he chortled, waving at the bottles littering the table.

"That is kind of you, French Frankie," Honas said after emptying his glass in a gulp for he was several drinks behind his companions.

"Me kind? Ho, ho," Coneaut chuckled. "Remember I am half-breed my friend, so I owe nothing to the white man who looks down on me as he does on your kind."

He refilled their glasses before he sat down. "To the white man, we half-breeds an' Quechans are like witches, but by God, they are all sonovabitches!" he said, sticking out his long tongue and wagging it back an forth like an overheated mastiff.

Honas merely grinned, but something about Coneaut's actions struck the usually grave Palma as being funny and he broke out into laughing at the swarthy Frenchman's antics.

Coneaut cocked his head, looking in surprise at Palma's outburst of laughter, then he, too, began to laugh raucously. Palma's reserve totally cracked and he began to screech in a high-pitched voice, laughing uncontrollably.

Tears of mirth were running down Coneaut's cheeks and he thumped his hands on his knees like a drum while he laughed. Then Honas broke into laughter at their antics, and it was good—for too long he had held in his sorrow until it was a poisonous thing. And for the time, a weight seemed to slide from his shoulders and the sounds of his mirth rose to match that of his friends.

Deep-throated, Coneaut's raucous laugh overshadowed Palma's high-pealed cackle, and Honas roared at his drunken companion's merriment. Wiping his eyes with the back of his hand, Coneaut straightened, then he got up and fetched a fresh bottle of brandy. He filled their glasses before he spoke: "An' now what does our leader plan to do?"

Honas shook his head. "I am not the leader. I dream now only of being a brave person."

"A brave man you already are, my son," Palma told him. "You are avenging our enemies like a true War leader."

"Thank you, my father, but the path is still long and perilous," he said.

"*Sacre Dieu*! I think I know now of what you speak!" Coneaut cried. "Five men have murdered you wife an' her mother, an' now two have already die!"

His dark eyes danced back and forth between Palma and the younger Quechan. "The condemned man, he smoked a last cigar, *n'est-ce pas*? An' the other man, he stretched my wire," he said matter-of-factly. "An' now you 'ave come to my store when the night she has fallen. By God, tomorrow I betcha, Doctor Botts will be called to the prison for there will be another dead man, no?"

Honas's lips held a tight smile. "Frankie dreams like a Quechan," he told Palma, nodding his head at Coneaut. Then his eyes set coldly and hate was a bitter glint on the hard lines of his face.

Desire for complete revenge was again pounding at him, a spur to driving him fiercely on but there was no satisfaction left in him. "You say there will be another dead man reported at the prison tomorrow—perhaps this will be so for their way is starless and steep, and the frailities of this life are many."

He took a swallow of the brandy Coneaut had poured before he continued: "A Quechan believes that the possession of life by the body is dependent only on the retention of the *metrao*."

"*Metrao*? What is that?" Coneaut asked.

"It is the principle soul," Honas explained. "You see, we believe that each person has many souls, but that death only occurs when the main soul leaves the body to go to our heaven, our place of the dead."

A wide-toothed grin spread over Coneaut's swarthy face. "An' you are helping these men find their, how you say—way to heaven?" he chuckled.

"I merely light the way for their main souls," Honas said, "For they have long ago lost their other souls."

Although it was hot in the windowless, murky room, the door was closed. Odors of fish and drying pelts cloyed the gloomy room while the three men sat in silence listening to the wild noises mingling with cantina music, as the sounds of Rincon Alley were reaching their zenith for the evening.

A rap on the door caused them to exchange glances before Coneaut arose unsteadily to his feet and walked to the door.

"By God, Sheriff," he cried, opening the door wider to reveal the Yuma lawman. "Welcome into my humble shop."

Waringer strode into the room, blinking his eyes in the dim light, his nose well aware of the coal-oil smell and the dim room's other odors.

"I thought I'd find you two here," he said, nodding at the Quechans seated at the table. "I came to tell you both what a fine job you did. Come by my office in the morning and I'll have some money for you. The Clip Mine people are going to ante up another hundred dollars for the recovery of the payroll."

"Sit down, Sheriff," Coneaut said, waving a hand toward the table. "By God, it is not everyday that I have such an august visitor. Weel you 'ave some brandy?"

Waringer nodded. He dropped his hat on the floor, then drew a chair to the table. He nodded his thanks when the Frenchman had filled a glass for him, then he held up the drink in a salute. The others joined him with a long pull at their glasses.

Waringer wiped the back of his hand over his mouth. He sat back in his chair while he studied the three faces seated across from him, his eyes touching each man in turn. "Been in here long?" he asked Honas.

"Ho, ho." Coneaut waggled a finger at the empty bottles setting on the table. "They have been here since the sun go down, Sheriff," he averred. "An' by god, since I have received a new case of brandy, we will be here till morning. You will join us, no?"

He indicated the half-empty bottle in his hand. "Will you have some more?"

Waringer held up his hand in refusal, his eyes noting the amount of brandy still in the bottle. "No thanks," he said. Picking up his hat from the floor, he got to his feet stiffly, weariness clutching his bones. "It's after midnight, and I've been on the go since sunup."

He walked to the door, then stopped, a friendly smile creasing his grizzled features. "Better you pass out first, Frankie, it's against the law to get Indians drunk."

Chapter Eleven

"I didn't want to disturb you last night, sir," Chief Guard Ben Harplee said while standing on the front porch of the superintendent's residence. Someone was up on the south wall last night. Guard Wilkins called out at exactly ten minutes after eleven. When I got there with lanterns, I found a stick about three feet long laying on the gravel. From the marks on the west wall, it looked like someone hurled it from over by the snake pit."

Tarbow's eyes narrowed at the mention of the solitary-confinement cell. "Did Wilkins see or hear anything before that?"

"He claims that he just heard the clatter when the stick bounced off the wall," Harplee said. "Naturally, I covered every inch of the rock hill but I didn't find any tracks."

"Was there anything unusual at the ventilator hole over the solitary-confinement cell?" the warden asked, apprehension beginning to build in his mind.

"No, sir." Harplee's head tilted inquiringly. "You mean like someone trying to tamper with it?"

The smell of breakfast bacon wafted from the kitchen behind him where his wife was starting to cook, but Joshua Tarbow was suddenly not hungry; an uneasy feeling pushed into his mind. He closed the door behind him and moved toward the steps as the ominous feeling grew.

"You hear any sounds out of Laustina while you were up on the hill examining the ventilator hole?" he asked hesistantly.

"Not really." A wry grin twisted the edge of Harplee's mouth. "You know how mad Jake gets, how he rants, but we didn't hear him yelling none. Anyway, I never paid any mind because I was trying to figure out who threw that stick."

Then the gut feeling hit Tarbow hard, and he cried out in trepidation as he started to run toward the prison gate. "Call out the guards! Get to the solitary-confinement cell!"

Tarbow stood shaking his head in resignation while Allison and Frettly dragged the heavyset Laustina from the cell and laid his swollen body on the gravel. Harplee eased himself from the cell opening, carring his rifle by the barrel.

"I killed two rattlesnakes in there, sir. Small ones they were, but deadly," he said matter-of-factly. "And we found two more larger rattlers in there, but they were already dead. Guess Jake killed them after they bit him."

Tarbow nodded numbly. He looked down at the bloated body of the three-fingered outlaw before he started to walk trancelike across the yard toward his office, knowing that he must act quickly before this got out of hand.

"Men." Superintendent Tarbow glared at the semicircle of guards seated in front of his desk. "I've called this meeting to inform you that we now have a Lowell Battery. The Gatling gun will stay in the east tower while the new Lowell will temporarily be assigned to the main tower."

A tenseness showed around Tarbow's mouth while he continued: "These unexplained deaths have got to cease! Starting tonight, and until further notice, I want lanterns on the walls at hundred-foot intervals, and I want a guard walking the top of each wall every night. From now on there will be no civilians allowed inside the compound without my personal approval, and that goes for those Indian trackers, as well."

He nodded at Botts seated in the corner of the room. "I'll account for the good doctor myself so he will not be your responsibility."

The guards exchanged glances, knowing full well that the superintendent was angry because of his concern for his job. Their eyes followed his pacing as he walked with head tipped forward, apparently absorbed in thought. The lines of his shoulders sagged dejectedly before he stopped.

"Harplee, arrange the men's schedules to include the walls, and have a copy on my desk for approval before suppertime," he directed the chief guard. "And have that new Lowell assembled at once. I want it loaded and manned up in the main tower before sunset, you hear? Dismissed!"

Surprised at the warden's suddenly tough stance, the guards filed silently from the office. Tarbow wiped a hand across his damp brow, then he tossed a quick look to where Botts sat complacently watching him, sensing that the doctor was wondering with tempered amusement how long it would be until his apprehensive orders resulted in unwarranted gunfire. Yet, when he reviewed past events, he was certain that he had chosen the proper course.

Botts had been summoned to the prison shortly after lunch and when he had arrived, he was promptly escorted to the solitary-confinement cell where Superintendent Tarbow and three guards stood at the open doorway of the cell, looking down at the body of Jake Laustina.

"That snake pit sure lived up to its name today," Frank Allison had quipped. "We found two dead rattlers, and then killed two more in there."

"Silence!" Tarbow roared, his agitated face was flushed darkly. "I want no more of that kind of talk!" His shoulders moved impatiently before he flicked tired eyes at the doctor. "Examine him, please," he said. "You stay here, Harplee, but the rest of you go take a break elsewhere."

Botts looked down at the bulky figure of Laustina stretched grotesquely on the ground, mouth frozen open in horror. He knelt, then carefully examined each bruised and swollen puncture mark on the lifeless outlaw. One of the huge hands still clutched a snake's head.

Botts stood up. "Looks like the snakes sent him into a frenzy of anger," he told them. "The man's strength was superhuman in his rage. From the looks of it, he tore the chain loose from that iron ring, then apparently, he used it like a whip to lash at the other snakes."

Tarbow nodded. "You're undoubtedly right, Doctor. If you're finished here, let's return to my office."

Botts shrugged. "There's no doubt that the death was brought about by the snakes."

"Did he die of snake *bites*?" Tarbow wanted to know, an uneasy feeling deep in his stomach.

Botts shrugged again. "In layman's terms—yes. Although with all his apparent exertion, it probably was due to cardiac arrest caused by the toxin's constriction of blood vessels to the heart."

Tarbow looked puzzled, so Botts added: "You see, there are two types of toxin in snakebites—neurotoxin and hemotoxin. These toxin vary from snake to snake. From the prisoner's general appearance, I'd say he was bitten a number of times where neurotoxins were predominant. Clinical effects include muscular pain, vomiting, and eventual respiratory and cardiac failure." He spread his fingers with finality. "You know how it is—when the old heart stops, that's it. I'll put the clinical effects on the Circumstances of Death Certificate for you."

Joshua Tarbow's eyes squinted at the sun, and the lines of his face tightened. He dabbed several times at the sweat that was on him, but the perspiration kept coming. He was a man who liked things safe—planned to the last detail. This was a measure of his professional capability—he acted, not out of fear but from a full knowledge of his job. And Tarbow had been a professional all his adult life. Not having any means of foreseeing the future, he somehow had to stop what was happening here, had to stop these mysterious deaths.

By Jupiter, he'd get to the bottom of this—no man would move in or out of this prison without his personal knowledge of it. That would bring things out into the open!

"Harplee," he growled irritably. "Get the body over to the carpenter shop and put clean clothes on him. I want him buried right after breakfast tomorrow."

Summer heat curled off the tamped gravel courtyard when Tarbow led the doctor back to the prison office. Yard prisoners lolled in the meager shade of the east wall while the clink of steel sounded from the blacksmith shop where convicts pounded out pick-points and sharpened shovels for the adobe crews.

Inside the office, Tarbow brought out two glasses and a bottle from a desk drawer. Normally not given to daytime drinking, he felt the need for spirits after what had transpired. Botts accepted the glass offered him and he moved to a chair.

Tarbow raised his glass for a quick gulp before he asked: "How do you think this happened, Rufus?"

The doctor shook his head, a faint grin tugging at his lips. "That's not my department, Josh. I'm hard-pressed just to know what killed him."

Tarbow drained his glass, then proffered the bottle to Botts. When the doctor nodded, he got up and moved around the desk to pour. "Someone, perhaps even one of my guards, dropped those snakes down through the ventilator hole, knowing that sooner or later, Laustina would get bitten," he said. "And right now, I'm beginning to suspect those two Quechans. This Honas Good seemed to resent Judge Morcum's mild sentencing of the murderers as not being severe enough."

Botts suddenly looked interested. "Did he have any specific accusations?" he asked.

"Well... He did say that he thought Morcum was as guilty as they, and that he, too, should have been sentenced. He seemed rather irate that the judge discriminated against the dead women because they were Indians. Raping and murdering white women would have drawn the death penalty."

"Hmmm. Then he didn't make any definite allegations or threats?"

Tarbow shook his head thoughtfully. "Not really, but he had a cold look on his face when he said: 'They have now all been sentenced.' Them was his words, just like he was passing judgment on them," Tarbow said. "I warned him against doing anything revengeful."

"That isn't very conclusive, Josh," Botts said. "You need something more tangible."

"How about circumstantial evidence? Now that I think of it," the warden added, "Honas was with Harplee outside the cell when Dwyer was killed."

"Harplee vouched for him, if I recall correctly."

"Yes, but I don't think Harplee really understood that he would have had to keep his eyes on the Indian every second to be able to vouch for him honestly," Tarbow said quickly. "He couldn't have watched Honas all the time because he was counting prisoners."

Botts nodded before taking a long sip at his drink. Then he sat back to watch the warden continue his pacing, not wanting to interrupt his thoughts.

"With the exception of the prisoner who was shot trying to lead a breakout the morning Fishel Dwyer lost his face, all the other men who died had something in common—

they were all involved when those Indian trackers' women were murdered," Tarbow said.

Botts looked out the office door, his mind selecting words carefully. Shimmering heat waves rose steadily from the graveled walkway for the late afternoon sun still blazed down unmercifully on the adobe and caliche walls.

He nodded. "That's the conclusion I came to shortly after they found Judge Morcum in that empty grave with a broken neck. Bliss had a similar look of terror frozen on his face. I didn't mention it before because I thought that you were on top of it, and I didn't want to interfere. Maybe what this Honas said was a threat after all!"

Tarbow's face changed, and a sudden light flared in his eyes with Botts's disclosure. He stopped pacing and a furrow creased his brow. He had lived too long by intangibles not to be willing to accept all things into this mystery, regardless of possible insignificance.

"You know, not being a townsman, I didn't give any consideration to Morcum's death," he said, now awakened to greater possibilities of murder. "I thought the drunken old fool just broke his neck stumbling around in an alcoholic stupor."

Botts shook his head thoughtfully. "You know that grave had been dug earlier the same day, for another man, but I believe Bliss Morcum would have ended up in that very grave, one way or another. Falling in just simplified matters," he exclaimed.

"Then there has to be a tie-in with what is happening here!"

"I think so, too," Botts said. "I think that Morcum was herded into that cemetery like a calf driven into a corral." He shrugged casually. "Naturally, the townspeople didn't have any reason to suspect a connection between his death and those of your convicts."

"But there certainly must be a connection now," Tarbow growled. Anger formed a flush on his cheeks. He didn't care to be taken for a fool by a couple of Indians, regardless of how valid their complaints. "Dwyer, Powers, Morcum, and now Laustina," he began to enumerate the deaths. "That means there are only two prinicipals left who were involved in that heinous drama."

"Carugna and Print." Botts said, supplying the names Tarbow was thinking. "Right?"

"Right!" Tarbow snapped. He paced back and forth in front of his desk while his thoughts began to jell and the self-righteous anger ebbed quickly from his face. He needed to sort things out in his mind. Then a satisfied smile wrinkled the corners of his mouth before he circled his desk and sat down.

"Thanks for your help, Rufus. I'll keep you informed of our progress in this matter," he said. He lowered his eyes and began shuffling papers on his desk as a means of dismissing the doctor.

"You do that, Josh," Botts said. He got to his feet and placed his glass on the desk. "I feel like I've got a stake in this matter since I'm the one who has examined all of the victims and signed those death certificates."

Tarbow nodded, smiling affably without speaking, not wanting to start a conversation that might encourage the doctor to stay. And after Botts had taken his leave, Tarbow poured another drink. God, it was hot, he mused. He raised his arm from the desk and several letters stuck to the perspiration on his wrist. Angrily, he shook the papers free with a flick of his arm. Now the damn heat was gluing things to him.

He leaned back in the chair—somehow, he had to plan a trap using the assumption that the Quechans were behind these senseless deaths. If he could solve the killings, or expose the Indians and their motives, the prison commissioners would overlook what had transpired.

That was it—he had to take the chance of catching the

culprits somehow. If the Indians were after the other two convicts, why not use them as bait in a trap?

Partially satisfied with the idea, Tarbow went home to supper, knowing that after the evening meal, he must return to his office so that he could concentrate on a plan....

Chapter Twelve

A cool breeze moving over the caliche riverbank behind the building swept warm air into the rear door of his office. Tarbow rested both elbows on the top of his worn oak desk and steepled his fingertips together, his mind in deep concentration. Print and Carugna, he thought, they were the last two actors in this grim drama staged here at the prison. Somehow, he needed to fashion his plan around them, a plan that used them as bait without their knowledge.

His mind stumbled ponderously over many ideas, but he discarded each as being too intricate. What he needed was something simple, something that exposed his bait in a seemingly routine manner, yet provided him with a backup for an ambush. Why not use the pending funeral? What would be more natural than two convicts burying their dead cell mate?

The more he tossed the idea around, the better he liked it. Print and Carugna could bury Laustina as a seemingly routine job. Other than the doctor, the prison didn't use Yuma facilities. Let the dead bury the dead.

But first he needed to go over the plan in his mind, needed to work out the details, then he needed some time for the word of the burial to get around.

Originally, he had proposed to bury the snake-bitten outlaw the first thing in the morning, but now he would have to change that. He'd tell Harplee to hold the body another day—that'd give the killers a chance to try something.

A hint of a smile touched his lips when he thought of the new Lowell Battery in the high main tower. It would be a real surprise because the gunner could cover all the ground along Penitentiary Road if trouble came that way, and no one would expect such firepower from that direction, even when most of the action, if the trap was successful, would be near the cemetery.

All the lines of his face pulled into a wry grin with the thought. Nothing ventured, nothing gained. First he needed to stop the proposed funeral, then he would spread the words for the Indians' benefit.

He put on his hat and stepped outside. Trapped heat on the low ceiling of the front porch almost stifled him and quickened his breathing while he walked to the guard's quarters in the gathering gloom of evening.

Harplee arose from a wicker chair in the off-duty dayroom when Tarbow entered. "What can I do for you, sir?" he asked quickly, for seldom did the superintendent come here except for an inspection.

Tarbow motioned the chief guard back to his seat, then he glanced around to see if they were alone. "I'm going to revise your schedule. I don't want Laustina buried until nine o'clock the day after tomorrow."

Harplee's brow wrinkled slightly, but he remained silent. Used to changes in orders, he knew that generally there was a good reason for the change.

"I have cause to believe that Honas Good and Palma are behind these odd deaths, and that they will try to kill Print and Carugna," Tarbow said seriously, his eyes searching for a reaction in the big guard's face. Finding none, he continued: "I want you to have two guards with Print and Carugna when they bury Laustina. I want two more guards under a tarpaulin between those stacks of adobe blocks you've got drying along the east road. Have another man down in the swine yard, and one on the east side of Cemetery Hill. Have them in place by six o'clock in the morning, and they will remain hidden with their rifles until trouble starts or they are relieved."

Harplee nodded his understanding. "Where do you want me?"

"You and I will be in the southeast tower so we can observe the action."

"May I ask, sir, what you expect?" Harplee asked.

Tarbow ran a thumb along his jaw before he answered. "I look for Honas and Palma to try to kill Print and Carugna. Give your men orders to shoot to kill if the Indians attack our convicts."

Emotion set the lines of the superintendent's face. "I suspect those two Indians of killing Dwyer, Powers, and Laustina. Doctor Botts feels that they caused Judge Morcum to break his neck in the dark," he said evenly. "We've got to stop them before they kill any more people over the murder of their wives."

"They can hardly be blamed for that, sir."

Tarbow eyed the guard coldly. "True, but look at it this way. The prison commissioners aren't interested in the motive, they will see it only as lax security if more convicts die. Both our jobs could be in jeopardy, you know."

Harplee thought that Tarbow's words sounded like an unwarranted threat; he had always been faithful, and had ever done his best. Yet he knew that Tarbow was quite worried about his own position, and he also knew that his job as chief guard really depended upon the superintendent's whims. If Tarbow feared for his job, then by gosh, he, too, better be concerned.

"By putting Print and Carugna out digging a grave, then burying Laustina, we make them highly visible and tempting targets. And the two Indians might think this was as good a time as any to finish the job," Tarbow explained. "But sooner or later, they have got to make their play, and because this is a routine duty, they won't suspect it is a trap."

"But if they don't attack, don't go for it," Harplee asked, "what then?"

Tarbow shrugged casually. "Well, we get Laustina buried. That's something he'll need by tomorrow anyway. After that, we'll just keep working on other traps."

Harplee nodded. "But knowing Honas, even if he thinks it's a trap, he won't be able to ignore such tempting bait. A chance to get at both men at once outside of the walls is a lot easier than breaking into prison to get only one at a time."

Tarbow was pleased to hear the big guard's answer, knowing he was a fearless man, and a crack shot with a 44–40 rifle. Harplee would take care of all the details in setting up the trap and briefing the other guards selected to take a part in the grim drama.

"If they try anything, we'll get them," Harplee said, then asked: "Have you discussed this with Sheriff Waringer yet?"

Tarbow shook his head. "No, and I don't intend to. I want to keep this plan and its execution strictly a prison affair. I will, however, mention to him about the change in burial plans. It would be well if tomorrow we spread the word in as many places as possible so them Indians will hear about it."

The conversation done, both men got to their feet, and at the door, Tarbow turned to express an idea that had just occurred to him. "When that ruffian, French Frankie, delivers our brandy supply, you make it a special point to see that he hears about the burial. He spends most of his time with the town's lower element, and he frequents many of the places where the Indians go."

Harplee touched two fingers to the brim of his cap. "I understand, sir."

"Good." Tarbow nodded. "I'll go over the plan more in detail with you tomorrow."

The big guard watched the superintendent move out into the moonless night before he resumed reading his newspaper.

"Aren't you afraid that the sheriff will arrest you for harboring two criminals?" Honas asked. The sputtering lamp was turned quite low and barely illuminated the back room of Coneaut's store.

"*Non*. He is not looking for you." French Frankie's swarthy face glistened in the dim light of the tepid room. "Neither of you. It is up to the superintendent to make the charges."

"And up to now he hasn't done so," Honas said, looking at Palma for his understanding. "But now you bring word that the man Laustina will be buried at nine o'clock tomorrow morning?"

"*Oui*, it was told to me by Harplee this morning," Coneaut said. "An' all day I hear this very same thing ever' place I go. But the rumors I hear are that the warden is looking for you."

The two Quechans exchanged glances. "I, too, have heard this spoken today," Palma said.

Honas took a small sip from the bottle of warm beer Coneaut had supplied earlier. "I'm sure that the warden now suspects us, my father," he said. "But he chooses not to involve the sheriff. According to law, he has jurisdiction over the prison and its grounds, so evidently he intends to catch us himself."

"*Oui*, that is so, but if Frankie can help, just let me know."

Honas shook his head. "That will not be necessary, my friend. Palma and I will take care of things." He tipped the bottle and drained his drink in a short gulp, then he arose. He offered his hand to the half-breed. "We go now."

"An' if the sheriff, he comes around tomorrow an' ask where you are?" Coneaut asked, a smile on his face after shaking Honas's hand.

A wry grin twitched the corners of Honas's lips as he stood in the darkened doorway. "Tell him that Honas and Palma went to a funeral."

"Or caused one," Coneaut whispered to himself after the door had closed.

Superintendent Tarbow yawned as he looked down toward the cemetery on the low slopes just east of the apiary. The swine yard lay just north of the burial grounds. He glanced at the stacks of adobe blocks drying just below the tower in which he and Harplee stood.

"Are all your men in place?" he asked.

The guard nodded. "Two of them are under that tarp between the second and third row of blocks. Got another man behind that hog trough in the corner of the pig pen. José Carala's in the scrub bushes on the low side of the cemetery."

Tarbow's eyes followed each of Harplee's directions but the men were so well concealed he failed to detect any of them.

"Wilkins is on the Lowell in the main tower. He's got the gun facing the cemetery road so he won't waste time turning it," the big guard explained. "The two men under the tarp are facing in opposite directions so they cover the road."

"Good, good." Tarbow nodded, pleased with Harplee's preparations. "Think we should have put two men up there?"

"Well, sir, with all that night patrol you ordered, we're pretty thin right now with available men. Wilkins is a good man, he can handle that gun alone. At nine o'clock sharp, Allison and Frettly will escort Print and Carugna out the sally port with Laustina's body in a pine box on a two-wheeled pushcart. Their pick and shovels will be on the cart with the body," Harplee explained. "The prisoners each will be wearing a leg weight in case they have to dodge around if there's fighting. Both Allison and Frettly will keep alert so that the prisoners don't escape."

Tarbow's lips pinched slightly. This was the only part of the plan he hadn't liked, not wanting to chance losing a prisoner by death or escape if something went awry.

"If we get the killers, I suppose I can justify any death that may happen. Escapees, we don't have to worry about very long, at least not with the desert all around us."

"That new Lowell gun in the main tower will protect the Yuma side, sir. Too bad we don't have more of them," Harplee said.

Tarbow snorted. "With the budget we have to operate this place, we're lucky to have the second gun. Eventually, when that new yard is completed, plans call for a women's area along the west wall, next to the insane cell. Perhaps by then we'll get another gun assigned instead of just loaned to us."

He was silent for a moment while his eyes swept the cemtery knoll, then he pulled his watch from his vest pocket. "Ten minutes to nine. You got the range to the cemetery?" He nodded at Harplee's rifle.

The big guard patted the barrel of his shiny rifle. "I've got the sights set for a hundred yards. I also had the other man estimate firing distances earlier."

"Good," Tarbow said. "Now all we can do is wait for the action to begin." He jerked a thumb eastward before adding: "I think that trouble will come from the slope around the cemetery, or from Prison Lane behind the wood yard."

"I had Allison and Frettly inspect that area right after breakfast."

"Good thinking," Tarbow complimented him.

"Here they come," Harplee interrupted the superintendent. He pointed to the pushcart rounding the east corner of the prison.

Print and Carugna walked slowly with a measured cadence, each holding the handle of the cart ladened with the large, unpainted pine box. A pick and two shovels were beside the coffin.

"Notice how Allison and Frettly keep right behind them, yet off to one side so there's little chance of making a run for it." The chief guard pointed to his men behind the convicts. "Learned that during the war at prison camps. A man can't run through a cart, so he has to take at least two steps to the side. That gives a guard warning his prisoner's going to try to make a break."

Tarbow was pleased with Harplee's efficiency. "You've done well, Ben. I intend to remember you in my reports to the commissioners."

"Thank you, sir."

A silence fell over the two men while they watched the slow movement of the funeral cortege down the dusty path leading toward the cemetery.

Suddenly the flat crack of a rifle sounded in the distance. Tarbow swiveled his head southeastward, striving to find some movement.

"What was that?" he asked nervously.

Harplee already had his weapon pointed in the direction of the shot, his keen eyes scanning Gila Slough, three hundred yards away. After several minutes, during which time both men stared at the dried slough, seeking danger in the withered reeds growing there.

Harplee straightened, relieving the tension. "Must be a kid shooting at frogs, or else it's a hunter."

The funeral procession had reached the end of the adobe yard and was turning toward the gravelly cemetery, undisturbed by the shot.

"Whew!" Tarbow whistled softly through his teeth. "I thought for a moment them Indians were trying to sniper our bait."

He wiped his forehead with a handkerchief, for already the sun was searing the blue clay ground below their tower perch. Those two men under the tarp between the adobe brick rows must be sweltering, he thought. Well, it shouldn't be much longer if there was, in fact, going to be an attempt on the prisoner's life.

Below them, the funeral cart had reached the cemetery, and Tarbow could see Allison pointing where Laustina's grave should be dug. He glanced back at the main tower and was comforted to see that Wilkins had tracked the cortege with the Lowell, the blue steel barrels had covered the procession all the way. Although the main tower was approximately four hundred and fifty feet from the cemetery, Tarbow wasn't concerned because the gun could spray the ground, and at such close range, little or no accuracy was needed.

He watched the two convicts unload the coffin, then pick up their tools. Print began to swing a pick, gravel chips flying, sweat shining on his shaven head and black face. Carugna shoveled loose material into a pile on the other side of the grave.

Tarbow watched the work progressing slowly while he again mopped his brow with the wet handkerchief. Feeling the tension ease, he became more aware of the heat building up in the tower, yet he forced his mind back to the panorama of the swine yard, apiary, and the cemetery where the men were working. He really did not know why, but he had expected an attack when the burial detail had first reached the cemetery, and now he felt that his plan had failed.

He wished that this tower was two-storied so that he could get a better view of the slough. Maybe after the new yard was completed, he could increase its height by making this a squad room, and adding another story.

He watched as Carugna climbed out of the waist-deep grave, and Print jumped in to take his turn at digging while the morning droned on. Allison and Frettly stood a short distance on either side of the grave, well out of reach of the tools if the convicts tried to overpower them.

Suddenly, his thoughts were shattered by the chattering of the new Lowell gun in the main tower, and he spun around to look at the revolving muzzles spouting flame toward the cemetery a hundred yards below.

Chapter Thirteen

On the last day of his life, Alexio Carugna's terror-stricken mind still betrayed him. During the past two weeks it had emitted danger signals where none existed, constantly provoking him to jump and cringe at the slightest sounds. Yet, when the Great Moment arrived, he was unprepared for it. Sleep escaped him to the extent that he became a hollow-eyed neurotic, obssessed with death by crucifixion.

After the garroting of Dalton Powers, he could not bring himself to attend Sunday chapel services in the mess hall because the makeshift pulpit for the visiting preacher had a wooden-cross design tacked to the front of it. Nor would he touch any of the adobe walls surrounding the prison yards, or look up when he walked near them.

Seldom did he emerge from his neurotic stupor to talk intelligently, and just as seldom did his cell mate, Hedgemon Print, attempt to converse with him beyond simple amenities.

Carugna sat on a lower bunk, his arms hanging between his knees when Allison rattled his heavy key ring against the bars of the door. Having spent a sleepless night, the noise brought him out of his gloomy reveries. Somehow he felt better today.

"Print. Wake up," he said. "It is time to eat."

The Negro on the top bunk rolled over onto his side to look down at his Mexican cell mate in surprise. This was the first time Carugna had spoken without prompting in several weeks.

"You ready to eat now?" Print asked, the sound of Allison rattling other cell bars still audible as he moved down the corridor shaking doors.

"*Sí*. Today I am hungry."

"'Bout time you is," Print growled. "All you been doin' is mumble-jumblin' you *Dios*."

Carugna turned brown eyes at Print. Strange, he thought, but today things looked brighter, nor did he feel as jumpy. He wet his dry lips, then ran a hand through his greasy hair. The inner fear was gone and he felt relieved.

Carugna rose to his feet and followed the large man from the cell. In the dining hall he ate hungrily, not looking right or left as usually did when he was in a crowd. He had just laid down his fork when Harplee's big hand dropped on his shoulder. Carugna stifled a cry, then dropped back on the bench when the guard restrained him, holding his shoulder.

"Easy, man," Harplee said. "I have a job for you and Print."

The guard took his hand from the Mexican's shoulder before nodding at Print. "I want you two in front of the carpenter shop right after breakfast. You're going to give Laustina his last ride, understand?"

Carugna shot Print a quick glance. The Negro's face was immobile for a moment, then he continued to chew.

At the carpenter shop, Harplee took the convicts inside to a back room. The body of Jake Laustina lay on a work table, his hands folded across his chest. "Get one of those boxes over here and lay it on the floor beside the table," Harplee said, pointing to several coffins standing on end against a wall. "Then put Jake in it."

A slight shudder went through Carugna when he took Laustina's feet, while Print raised the dead man's shoulders. He had never touched a dead body and the stiffness of the three-day-old corpse surprised him. And the eyes were still open.

Oh God, why hadn't someone closed Jake's eyes when he died? Then he recalled hearing that if a person died with his eyes open, they couldn't be closed unless an undertaker wired them. Fear began to creep into his system, and he cast furtive glances at the dead man who once had tried to kill him. Print hammered the lid into place while Carugna stood fidgeting.

"Put the box on that two-wheeled pushcart, along with a pick and shovel. Then you two stand by with the coffin at the sally port. The guard will let you out at nine o'clock sharp," Harplee said. "Allison and Frettly will be outside the gate to escort you down the hill; and to make sure that you don't decide to run, there'll be a ten-pound lead bracelet locked around your ankle."

Carugna helped lift the heavy coffin onto the pushcart, then loaded their tools. They wheeled the cart to the gate in silence, then listened to Allison and Frettly chat with the gate guard.

"Think there'll be any trouble?" the gateman asked.

Allison shrugged. "Don't know, but the old man is sure jittery. He's up in the south tower with Harplee. He's got four men hidden out there somewhere, that's all I know."

Carugna looked at Print, the guard's talk gradually having a meaning for him. Someone was going to try to kill them while they were burying Laustina.

"Trouble? What trouble is there going to be?" he asked Print. "Is someone going to make a try at us?"

But Print never got to answer. "Shut up!" Frettly snapped. "No more talking."

Carugna's eyes pleaded with Print for an answer, but he gave no recognition of the question. Carugna wiped a palm across his forehead, yet in spite of the heat he felt a chill tingle his spine.

"All right, let's go," Allison called. The gateman swung one of the big gates open and waved them out.

A sudden quiet seemed to pervade the air when the pushcart moved along the east wall. Hot air suddenly enveloped Carugna; he began to breathe deeper, and a fear hovering in the pit of his stomach began to creep upward. His little eyes flicked back and forth, sensing danger as the tingling sensation in his spine began to climb. Why did he suddenly think of death? Wasn't he safe with Allison and Frettly walking alertly behind them, and hadn't the guard said that four other armed men were watching?

Safe from what—who? His mind spun—who was he afraid of? Yet deep inside, he knew otherwise—he had robbed and killed, ever sinning against God. And now he would pay for it.

Suddenly a shot cracked in the distance. Desperately he clutched the cart handle, not daring to release it for fear that he would run, then bullets from the two guards behind him would cut him down. Print's measured stride contin-ued, and he dragged stumbling feet to stay with the cart.

"*Madre de Dios*. It is a signal," he gasped. He could feel the sweat running down the inside of his cotton jacket. His throat was rasping dry.

"Stop your mumble-jumble, Mex," Print snapped. "Your God ain't got no business heah."

"Cut the chatter, you two!" Frettly ordered loudly.

When Carugna realized that nothing had happened, he began to breathe deeper again. They stopped the cart, then Allison kicked the toe of his boot into the gravel. "Here's where you can plant him, so unload the box."

Somehow he felt better when the work began; keeping busy kept his mind from the fear lurking in his gut. Print handed him a shovel and he began to scrape away at the gravelly ground. When Print had loosened a large rectangle of soil, Carugna began to shovel with a vigor. His mind flowed free and clear as his fears evaporated; and the toil began to tax his muscles while he threw shovelsful of dirt from the grave.

"Let me in there, now," Print said. "You up to you waist now already."

Perspiring, but glad for the change, Carugna scrambled out of the pit. He stood watching while Print jumped into the pit, then his eyes traveled to the guards who had moved back from the grave, not wanting to be within reach of the dirt the big Negro was throwing.

A steady popping sound rippled behind him and he turned. Paralyzed, he watched an advancing line of spurting gravel speeding at him before his mind recognized the danger.

"*Madre de Dios*!" he screamed. Twenty chunks of lead hammered into his body, smashing him senseless into the grave on top of the crouching Negro.

Print held Carugna's body as a shield, keeping himself well below the edge of the grave while the firing continued.

"Down, down!" Allison cried. "The tower gun is goin' crazy!" He ran forward and threw himself behind a gravel mound, rifle to his shoulder. "We've got to stop whoever it is!"

Frettly yelled: "Cover me!" He raced forward while Allison fired four shots in rapid succession at the figure manning the Lowell in the tower. When Frettly reached cover, he signaled the other guard to move, then he sent protective fire at the sniper still churning gravel from the edge of the grave.

Then suddenly a hush fell over the scene when the Lowell became silent. Acrid smoke drifted beneath the roof while cries from the main gate alerted other guards. Allison and Frettly, running up the slope to the tower, were joined by guards who had crawled from under the tarpaulins in the adobe yard.

Rifles at the ready, the two guards cautiously mounted the stairs to the tower, and slowly crept upward. Peering over the banister, Allison could see no one near the gun. He motioned Frettly to follow, then he stepped quickly forward. Wilkins lay on the floor moaning, both hands holding his head.

"What happened?" Allison asked. "You all right?"

Wilkin's hat lay under the Lowell gun's carriage and he reached for it, then sat up before he answered. "I'm all right," he mumbled, "but I don't know what happened."

"Stand back, stand back," Harplee ordered the guards crowding the stairway when he and the superintendent pushed their way through the men milling around the dazed Wilkins.

Tarbow helped the man to his feet. "What happened? Who fired that gun?"

"I—don't know, sir," Wilkins said. He winced when he tried to put on his hat. "I was keeping the new gun pointed at the burial cart just like you ordered. When they got to the cemetery, I drew a bead on them working. That's all I remember, sir."

He felt the lump on his head and winced again. "Guess someone clobbered me from behind."

Tarbow quickly moved to the railing and anxiously looked down at the cemetery. There was no movement there, nor could he see anyone. "What became of Print?" he cried. "Where is he?"

"Why he was still down in the grave," Allison gasped. "I thought he got hit like Carugna, maybe killed. Anyway he was still in the grave when we left to get that gunner."

Then Tarbow saw a guard, his rifle at the ready, moving in from the swine yard. Choking back a curse, Tarbow waved the men away. "Harplee, have someone take Wilkins to the doctor, then you and Allison come with me. The rest of you fan out and search the outer grounds for whoever was in the tower!"

The warden led Harplee and Allison in a brisk walk down to the cemetery. They found the bloody, mangled body of the Mexican convict lying humped at the bottom of the bloody grave.

"Dammit!" Tarbow growled. "Print got away during the shooting." His eyes squinting against the sun, he looked toward the slough. "Where'd you say your other guard was posted?"

"Come, I'll show you." Harplee stepped out rapidly, Tarbow and Allison walking in his wake. On the far side of the hill they found the unfortunate guard, lying facedown, the back of his head crushed. A bloody pick handle was in the sand at his feet.

"His rifle's gone," Harplee said, shaking his head in disgust. "That means Print is armed. That pick handle is from the prison—see our brand on it?"

"Allison, you look around the slough," Tarbow growled. "That shot we heard was some sort of signal. Ben, you form a group to go after Print. Take Chato with you, and I don't care if he kills the black...." He paused, then wagged his head. "I mean...shoot to kill if you have to," he amended his order.

"This place is *really* becoming a 'Hellhole,'" Doctor Botts said. "Your man Hack died of a crushed skull, and the little Mexican was riveted from knee to scalp with lead slugs. That Lowell gun certainly made ground meat outa him."

Tarbow sat with both elbows on his desk, his fingers steepled in his favorite position. "Evidently, when the shooting began all my men concentrated on the tower. Print probably escaped when the guards converged their fire on the gunner."

He tapped his fingertips against his teeth before continuing. "Somehow, someone overpowered Wilkins, then fired at the convicts. I say that because both guards down there reported that the gunfire was directed only at the two prisoners at the grave. Only Carugna was hit, but he got the full blast."

"What about your other man?" Botts asked. "The outlying guard on the hill?"

"José Carala?" Tarbow tapped his teeth with his extended fingers again. "Well—either Print got behind him while he was occupied and crushed his skull with a pick handle so he could take his rifle, or someone else did it. We found a pick head in the grave with Carugna, so I think it was Print."

"Someone else?"

"Remember we were talking about the Quechans," Tarbow said. "Well, there are two of them. Just before the pushcart carrying Laustina's body started down the hill, a shot sounded over near Gila Slough. Now I'm wondering if it was a signal. You see, a man located there could see the funeral cortege coming down the hill."

"Why would a signal be needed?" Botts asked, not understanding the direction of Tarbow' discussion.

"A man hiding at the water's edge below the hill could not be seen, but neither could he see the funeral cortege when it started down the hill. If an accomplice signaled the start of things, then the man, particularly if he was an Indian, could scramble up that caliche hill and sneak alongside the guard barracks and creep up the tower stairs with little or no chance of being detected."

From the expression on the superintendent's face, Botts knew the man was thinking out loud, so he remained silent.

"Wilkins was alone in the tower with orders to track every step of the two convicts and the cart. Keeping his gun on them required concentration, so he wouldn't be as apt to hear a stealthy man behind him until it was too late."

"Then you think it was one of those Indians who fired the Lowell battery?"

Tarbow nodded. "Probably was Honas. He's young and moves like a wraith. And even though he concealed it well, his hate is still there."

"Well, if that's the case, he's only got one more convict to go," Botts said lightly. "But he'll have to catch Print, and that may not be easy."

Tarbow was in no mood for levity. "He caught him once, and no doubt he'll catch him again."

"Then that'll be the end of your problem."

"No, it's another start. Honas has broken the law by committing murder. Now he must be brought to justice," the superintendent said angrily.

"Anyway, he'll find Print a different fish to catch. He's not too long out of the jungle. He reminds me of a sleek panther," Botts told him.

Tarbow lowered his hands to his desk, then studied them a moment. "Print's not in the jungle now, but knowing who is after him, he'll use all the cunning at his command."

"You think Honas will go after him?"

"Yes. It just happened that when he knocked Wilkins on the head, Carugna was the only convict in the open. Honas didn't have time to wait for a shot at Print, so he just sprayed the Mexican. Print kept his head down until my men started to advance on the tower. Knowing that the gunner would be busy, Print evidently took off over the hill until he saw Carala. Somehow he killed the guard and took his rifle before he escaped."

"This Palma, what about him?" Botts asked. "If he gave the signal from the slough, he was near enough to see what transpired."

"True, maybe Palma's already on Print's trail," Tarbow said. "His hate is just as great as Honas's."

"Now what?"

"Well…I guess I'll have to call in the sheriff because Honas was not a regular employee—a sworn-in guard. As such, I have no control over him, but because he no doubt will be after Print, I'm sending Harplee and three men, too. Whether they go with Waringer or not is immaterial, they are still going to go after our prisoner."

Sheriff Waringer sat quietly listening to the superintendent's explanation of events surrounding Carugna's murder and Print's escape.

"I'll have a small posse ready to go within the hour," Waringer said. "But we won't have a tracker. Neither Chato, nor any of the other Indians will go against the Quechans."

"Harplee and two men will accompany you from here, Sheriff," Tarbow said. "You can be in charge of the group, but I want Print brought back here. You can have the Indians if you catch them—after they are tried, they'll end up here anyway."

"Agreed, Warden," Waringer told him. "My men will meet your guards at the cemetery, and we'll go from there."

Chapter Fourteen

Wearing moccasins, denim pants, and a brown shirt, it took Honas Good almost an hour to work his way along the bank of the Gila River. Having entered the water well before dawn, he pulled himself slowly along the river's edge, using grass and bushes for handholds to propel him. Swimming, he had decided, was too risky; it might draw someone's attention if they were looking at the river.

Where the underbrush had thinned, he slid gracefully underwater swimming slowly downstream until the brush again furnished concealment. When he drew nearer to the prison, the caliche rose from the sandy soil, forming the large expanse of Prison Hill.

He moved to the steep bank, clinging to jutting rocks while he surveyed the terrain. Just around the next clump of bushes was the small building housing the pump that forced river water up into a circular stone tank beneath the main guard tower. He knew that the guard barracks were located at the top of the bank above the pump house. Now was the time to leave the river. He crawled into the brush at the base of the caliche bank, and settled down for the long wait.

The stars were fading into the gray light of dawn when he looked eastward toward the Gila where it cut across the neck of the valley before swirling into the mighty Colorado.

He knew that most of the prison's water came from the Gila, a much slower moving body of water. Water from the Colorado was heavy with sand and was brownish in color, but fortunately the pump inlet received most of its water from the Gila current before it got mixed with the darker water. Even so, the prison had to settle most of the water before it was used, due to the soil carried from the mountains. On both sides of the Gila, however, the desert was parched and dusty, and the sandy wastes were harsh and unforgiving.

Honas lay back, his head propped against a bush, and watched the yellow streaks in the eastern sky, harbingers of the sun soon to cover this land. He could see a beauty here, a land with grandeur that only an Indian could really appreciate. But this land also held a challenge, a dare against holding a place in it. A constant battle with the sun and sand was never easy; it was fight enough—man didn't need his own kind to fight against.

Honas stirred within the shade of the underbrush for the sun was now positioned near the time he anticipated. Ready for the morning's heat and dust, he reveled in the thought of the vastness of the land of his fathers, the land to which he would soon be forced to return.

Off to his left the flat-crack of a rifle sounded, the noise rolling sharply across the water. Palma's signal, the funeral party was starting down the dusty road to the cemetery.

Quickly he checked the knife in his belt, a weapon with a long, heavily weighted handle, then he parted the brush and began a rapid climb up the steep caliche bank. He knew that it was imperative that he reach the tower before the funeral procession got to the cemetery because all eyes would be following the burial cart.

Having watched numerous prison funerals, he was aware of the route and the approximate time it took to get the body to the cemetery. The rough caliche bank, weathered

by many centuries, provided easy footholds for his moc-
casined feet.

At the top of the bank he paused in a crouch, ears
keened for sound, then he ran quickly forward along the
east side of the barracks. Off to his right, nestled among
several drooping trees, stood the superintendent's house.
Then crouching low, he sprinted soundlessly across the
open ground to a low picket fence surrounding the tower.

So far, so good, he thought. Then, taking a deep breath,
he stepped over the fence and mounted the low dirt bank
around the partially exposed water tank. The tower floor
formed a platform over the top of the masonry tank. Now
hidden from view, except by the empty barracks behind
him, Honas stood up slowly.

Even with his back turned, the familiar figure of Elmo
Wilkins was recognized at the Lowell gun. He knew Wilkins
to be an able but slow-witted guard with many years of service. Shifting the knife to the rear in his belt, where it
would be less apt to make a noise, Honas drew himself up
over the platform. Getting stealthily to his feet, he grasped
the knife from his belt. Holding it so that most of the handle was exposed, he moved silently behind the unsuspecting Wilkins who was leaning forward intently, one hand on
the Lowell's crank, and the other hand on the trigger. The
angle of his position exposed the back of his head better
than Honas had expected.

Down crashed the weighted handle of the knife and
Honas caught the guard by his collar with his left hand,
easing him to the floor. Doubling his fist, he sent a short
jolt against Wilkins's jaw to insure him a little more time
for his task.

He quickly returned the knife to his belt and hovered
over the gun, looking at the sights. Wilkins had done a fine
job of tracking the convicts, for the weapon was already
pointed where the burial party stood.

He was surprised how long it had taken him to reach his objective and get ready to act, for the convicts were already at work digging the grave.

A tenseness lay over the grim scene below, like knowing that dynamite was going to explode, yet not being quite certain where. An inner sense prompted him to act. He watched while Carugna stood in front of the grave. Unfortunately only a portion of the black convict was exposed, but he knew that he must chance it; hopefully he would get them both.

The handle turned and gravel spat within thirty feet of the grave. He raised the gun slightly—saw the bullets hammer Carugna backward into the grave on top of Print. He kept turning the crank, keeping the bullets chewing up dirt and gravel at the edge of the grave until the clip was empty.

Chips of wood splintering from a corner post brought him back to reality. The guards were firing at him while they advanced. With a running leap he sailed from the platform down to the bank, and with another jump cleared the picket fence. Crouching low he raced across the open ground and sailed down the bank in two jumps, landing in the bushes. Quickly, he crawled through the underbrush and eased himself into the water. Taking a deep breath, he swam beneath the surface until he was forced to come up for air. Then he gulped another breath and again swam underwater for another hundred feet before surfacing.

When he deemed that he was a safe distance beyond the prison property, he came out of the river. Emptying water from his moccasins, he drew them back on. Unharmed, except for scratches and minor bruises, he began to trot along the river for his meeting with Palma.

And on the last day of their lives two men awoke under different circumstances. Hedgemon Print, the huge son of a West Indies slave, rolled over on his bunk when Carugna called for him to awake. He was tired of the Mexican's whining and mumble-jumble, and so he was glad when the man had receded into a witless stupor. Several times Print had been almost driven the assailing his cell mate, but he had managed to hold himself in, not wanting to end up in the solitary confinement pit—especially after what had happened to Laustina.

Snakes in that cell meant only one thing—someone was eliminating each of the men who had been a party to the rape and murder of the Quechan women. That was it—the two Indian trackers were getting their revenge, not this God Carugna was always mouthing about. Spirits and hexes were beyond him, but men—even Indians trying to kill him—were something he could understand, something he could get his teeth into. When the damn mystery was stripped away—it was man to man, and he was unafraid.

When Harplee ordered him and Carugna to report to the carpenter shop to bury Laustina, he was noncommittal. When the gateman, later, had asked Allison if there was going to be trouble, the guard's answer confirmed what he had already suspected.

Damn, if there was going to be an attempt on his life, he would welcome the chance to meet it out in the open. The Mexican, too, suspected something was amiss and began to whine. He had shrugged off all his cell mate's questions, however, pushing the cart boldy forward with a measured cadence.

The crack of a rifle further affirmed that there was a plot brewing, but he moved resolutely forward in spite of Carugna's begging. After twenty minutes of digging the feeling grew stronger within him, and he started to become apprehensive, the tense waiting grinding an edge to his nerves.

Better he get into the pit and dig, he thought, not wanting the guards to see his increasing nervousness. No sooner had he exchanged places with Carugna, then he heard the pop-pop of bullets stitching across the gravel and he sank quickly down into the grave.

He felt Carugna's body fall across his back, felt the warm blood running across his sweaty form while dirt and gravel rained down on him. He heard the guard's boot steps running toward the embankment when the Lowell Battery stopped chattering its song of death.

He pushed Carugna's body away, then he peered cautiously over the rim of the grave. Both guards were running toward the tower, firing their rifles as they ran.

He grabbed the pick, and holding it by the head, stamped the handle into the ground until the head slid free. Carrying the handle like a club, he scrambled out of the grave, and began an awkward run up the slope, the lead weight curtailing his stride.

Suddenly he saw a guard known as Carala rise from behind a mesquite bush, his back half turned. Print swung the pick handle in a vicious arc, catching the guard on the skull. Down went the surprised man who had been trying to watch Gila Slough, and the footsteps behind him.

Quickly Print swung the club again and again until the guard was dead, then he dropped the handle and grabbed the rifle. Still crouching, he saw the movement in the bushes off to his right, then he sank to one knee, leveling the 44–40 at the brush.

From the profile he recognized the Indian as one the trackers called Palma. He's the big-titted squaw's man, he thought. Print squeezed the trigger and saw him pitch forward. Now maybe he and his woman would be together in whatever heaven these people had. He walked quickly over to the fallen Quechan and nudged him with the toe of his boot.

The bullet had ripped a ragged hole through Palma's side under his armpit, the slug passing through his heart. Print looked at the dead Quechan's older model rifle and rejected it. Returning to the dead guard, he stooped and unfastened Carala's leather cartridge canister from his belt, then bounded awkwardly into the brush, striving to put distance between him and the prison.

A half hour later Print cautiously approached the same prospector's shack where he and the other three escapees had visited to chisel off their chains so long ago. Through the shimmering heat waves, he saw that the door to the shack still hung askew from one hinge when he broke it. Evidently the prospector had never returned.

Boldly he trotted to the deserted shed where he found a broken and rusted saw blade. Hell, he thought, even a wood-saw will cut lead. Ten minutes later he had cut the weight thin enough so that he was able to twist it loose using a ragged chisel and a bent screwdriver.

Knowing that there was no water or food on the premises, he began to trot toward the river. He needed to refresh himself—dirt and Carugna's blood caked his sweat-drenched clothing. At the Gila river he took a quick plunge, then drank deeply of the cool water. Squinting at the sun, he took a southeasterly bearing and walked rapidly.

The sun was a molten orb focusing on Print's shaven head, and he cursed himself for not having taken Carala's cap, or even picked up his own blood-covered hat from the grave. Heat from the sky hammered down on him, and reflected back from the sand, stealing his breath away. He had once heard that this Sonoran desert often reached 150 degrees, and he felt that today was one of those days.

His ankle began to throb where the lead weight had chafed it raw while he walked. Suddenly he realized that he was not moving very fast, and that the rifle's weight was becoming noticeable. He licked his dry lips and spurred himself to a faster pace through the endless sand.

It was late afternoon when his dragging feet came to a halt. Rifle hanging, stock to the ground, he peered behind him through burning eyes. Here and there long scrub bushes hugged the torturing sand and the shimmering heat waves radiating from the ground distorted his vision.

Hell, right now he couldn't make out a man from a bush anyway. Why keep looking? Besides, when they came there'd be many of them, and with horses, too. Yet something akin to cold fear lay in the recesses of his mind, and he knew it had nothing to do with a posse.

Then his eyes caught a flutter on a waist-high cactus off to his left. Shuffling quickly forward he found an arrow sunk deep into the cactus barrel. It was a short piece of yellow ribbon tied to the shaft that had attracted his attention. Quickly his eyes swept the brush again before he saw the second arrow partially driven into the ground with its wisp of yellow ribbon visible. Yellow ribbons! Fear clamped his chest like a giant band.

Honas Good's young wife had yellow ribbons braided in her hair that fateful day! He began to run off to the right, frantically eager to put distance between him and the fearful arrows.

Gulping hot air into overworked lungs soon reduced his movement to a stumbling pace before he stopped. Feebly he wiped a hand over his dry mouth, then tried to lick the sweat from the back of his hand. Throat rasping, he began to walk again, his steps dragging weakly. The sun had reached the horizon when he revived from a somnambulistic stupor.

He stopped and gazed bleary-eyed at the scrub trees ahead. Trees meant that water was somewhere beneath that burning sand, and he shuffled rapidly forward. There it was, a tiny pool of water nestled between the trees. Print dropped to his knees and lay with his face in the water and when he had drunk the puddle dry, he scraped deeper into the sand until more water bubbled up. Pieces of adobe and sticks mingled with sand clogging the well were pushed aside by Print in his frenzy to get more water.

His thirst quenched, he got to his feet and peered around, for there was something familiar about this place. Adobe blocks were scattered around, half covered by sand, and a corner of a structure was still intact against the ravages of the desert winds. The brush roof had long since blown away, along with other debris. Then his glance came back to the well at his feet; this had once been a thriving well, not a mere water hole partially blocked and blown over with sand. Then an eerie feeling like a frosty finger touched his spine. This had been the homesite of those Quechan trackers and the two women he had helped ravish and kill!

Once again he glanced furtively around at the purple gloom settling over the land. Was there someone still out there, someone tracking him? He felt cold in spite of the heat still radiating up from the sand. But he knew that he had to rest and recharge his waning energy. Water would help and he was glad he had been able to find some. He would sleep a few hours, then drink his fill of the precious water before leaving. Even though he had no canteen his rejuvenated strength should carry him to Mexico by tomorrow afternoon.

But tired as he was his superstition would not let him sleep near the ruins of the *jacal*. He curled up on the sand a short distance away, the rifle at his side, before a wearied sleep overtook him. Soon in his troubled dreams the dead women began stirring with the desert wind now starting to blow.

Several times he jerked awake with a start at the low moaning of the wind, which at times sounded like curses, then, rising in pitch, it sounded like the lamented wailing of women in sorrow. Straining his eyes into the shadowy darkness, he keened his ears striving to determine the source of every new sound chilling him. And each time he awakened he hurriedly sat up, until exhausted, his strength deserted him and he slept.

Chapter Fifteen

But on the last day of the other man's life fate was not less harsh. Hedgemon Print awoke with a start. Grabbing his rifle he got to his feet, striving to see that which had awakened him, but he could see nothing in the moonless gloom.

He cocked his head against the blowing wind, but could hear nothing above the whisper in the trees. A light shiver passed over him when he looked toward the adobe ruins that once had been an Indian hovel. Still tired, his mind began to function—better he leave here at once now that he was awake, but first he needed to drink his fill of water.

He searched around in the dark but couldn't seem to find the well. Maybe it had sanded over, he thought, but the wind hadn't been that gusty. Regardless, he had to have water. On hands and knees he crawled until he found the wet spot on the sand, then he scooped with both hands until a small pool formed. He drank eagerly, by cupping his hand into the water. Phtew! He spat the foul-tasting water from his mouth.

He spat again before smelling his hand. The strong odor of urine assailed his nostrils. Someone had soiled the water!

"Damn it!" he cursed angrily; someone had fouled the well so that he couldn't drink. And no wonder he had such a difficult time finding the well; someone purposely had scraped over it after urinating in the water.

Latent fear suddenly shot through him—if someone was close enough to besmirch the water, they were close enough to kill him! He raised the rifle quickly. Any man trying to take him now would die in the attempt, he told himself. His hand reached to lever a cartridge into the chamber but found only a twisted stub of metal where the lever had been.

Fear slashed through Print like lightning. Someone had fouled the well, then had surreptitiously taken his rifle and broken off the lever before returning it to his side. Why hadn't that someone killed him while he lay sleeping? What manner of man could do this? Where was he now?

Nerves taut, he spun around wide-eyed, staggering while he stared into the shrouding gloom. But he could see nothing in the darkness, so he dropped the useless rifle and began to run clumsily as though possessed. When his lungs seemed ready to burst, he stopped and looked behind him in vain.

Sides heaving, he strained his ears for sounds of pursuit but heard nothing. He began walking slowly, gulping air until his breath fitfully returned. When the eastern sky began to lighten, he quickened his shuffling pace. The wind had died and warm air was already beginning to move upward from the sand when the sun neared the crest of the distant hills. He glanced quickly behind him again but the horizon was clear. He took another bearing for the direction and was chagrined to find he had wasted most of the night stumbling eastward instead of moving toward Mexico.

He licked dry lips, wishing that he had drank more water while he had the chance last night. He moved in a southerly direction with dragging steps as fast as he was able, trying to cover as much distance as possible before the blazing heat began.

Damn those two Indians, he thought. Why hadn't they minded their own business and not tracked him and Laustina that fateful day they had robbed the stagecoach? Why were they helping a damn sheriff, of all people, anyway? He had nothing against Indians except that they were a white man's pawn when they took up tracking for a living. Begrudgingly, he admitted they were good. Damn them all anyway, he cursed to himself, hadn't they found him and Laustina within twenty miles of the stage robbery?

Again he glanced nervously behind but nothing moved in the early morning light. The heat pressed down on him with surprising suddenness when the sun finally crested into the open. Feet dragging, his tongue thick and dry, Hedgemon Print kept moving. Far ahead lay the purple-blue hills of Mexico and safety if only he could reach them before the full heat of the desert engulfed him.

He would have to get to water in order to keep up this pace or he would surely die. Death comes to everyone, he thought, even to that bull of a man, Laustina. But not me, he growled to himself, at least not yet. Then thinking of bulls, he recalled a bullfight he had once witnessed in Mexico a long time ago.

Even though he was a violent man, he had somehow hated the bullfight. A fight was a fight but he hadn't liked the way those Mexicans wouldn't stand up to the bull, and he hadn't liked the way they had danced around while they stuck the animal at the top of his shoulders with their barbs before running away from him. The matador, however, had been a little different. He had been more clever but he stood in front while he challenged the bull, goading him gradually into outraged recklessness when he could endure no more. Finally, after the beast had been tormented until his strength was gone, the matador held his ground. He had met the bull's lethargic charge and deftly slid a sword downward into the animal's heart.

Suddenly a chill swept through him—wasn't this exactly what was happening to him? Wasn't he being goaded like a bull into exhausting anger and made ready for the kill?

He stumbled while frantically looking behind again, striving to see through the shimmering desert. Damn it, where was this cunning matador he couldn't see? Was he out there now?

Staggering onward once more, Print's feet still moved but his mind was beginning to sink into a torpor. Throat raw, his lips cracked, he noticed that the terrain had changed. Long, shallow-fingered draws and washes stemmed out from the hills. He cast another lingering look over his shoulder but nothing moved save for the shimmering heat waves above the scrubby sage.

Yet he felt that someone was out there—that matador who was relentlessly goading him on. Goading, goading, goading! The sounds now coming from deep within his chest were merely croaks as he cursed his unseen nemesis.

His brain numbed, he shuffled his feet, step by step, gasping for air through dried throat and mouth. He staggered onward. How little or how long he had been walking was unknown but suddenly a great haze seemed to appear in front of him and he halted.

He reared back his head. It took a long moment for the scene to penetrate his befuddled mind—the hills just in front of him were on the Mexican border!

"I...have...won...," he cackled hoarsely. Only a few more yards and he would be safe in Mexico. Then he would have to find water, and soon, for he was growing steadily weaker.

Just like that bull in the arena, dragged slowly through his mind.

He staggered forward before sliding helplessly down into a ravine in a heap, but when he reached the top of the other side, he would be in Mexico! Head down, with eyes fixed on the sand, he slowly began crawling on hands and knees to the top of the other bank before something caused him to stop.

His brain gradually registered when his eyes took in the knee-length moccasins a few steps in front of him. Numbly, he raised his head. In front of him stood the silent matador who had been harrying him these many miles across the blazing desert. Terror froze his very mind!

Naked, except for a leather loincloth, the awesome Quechan stood, his face painted in a ceremonial blood-red death mask with a black stripe leading down across his forehead and nose. A bright yellow palm print was stained on his chest near his heart, with two thin black horizontal lines through the palm print.

Startled, Print wearily raised his eyes to the foreboding long-handled knife the Quechan had drawn from his loin-cloth before moving slowly forward. With a hoarse cry of despair, Print pushed to his feet to grapple with Honas Good. His left hand grasped the warrior's knife wrist, while the Quechan clutched the Negro's other wrist.

Muscles bowed and knotted, they stood face to face straining their sinews, trying to bow each other. Perspiration flowed down Print's face as they locked in a duel of brute strength, but the goading of the matador had taken its toll. In his weakened condition, Print's strength slowly gave way to the relentless pressure of the painted Quechan.

The knife moved slowly downward. Veins, like ropes, stood out on Print's forehead as his legs gradually bowed under the Indian's steady determination and his knees dipped toward the ground.

His throat was too raw to gasp for air before the tip of the Quechan's long blade touched flesh between his left collarbone and back muscles. *Mercilessly goaded and now stabbed just like the bull in the arena*, ran through Print's mind before Honas lunged the blade downward in a power-ful thrust.

Print's mouth flew open, but pinched shut tightly with-out uttering a sound. The long blade had reached Print's heart and he sagged to both knees in the sand. After a moment, Honas withdrew his knife and Print's body fell face downward. He wiped the knife blade clean on the convict's striped uniform before he straightened.

He looked once in the direction of the land of his forefathers with deep regeret for all his losses. His wife Avita was back there dead; Palma his friend was dead, and so were all his dreams for life.

It was then he realized that maybe he had misinterpreted his dreams, for after all, he was still a Quechan. He wasn't meant to have wealth or live in the world of the white man. As in his dreams, he would never be able to hold on to his worldly goods. He would constantly lose them along the way.

He turned his eyes back toward the hills of Mexico and his mind moved to the past. Somewhere, hiding in those hills, there were still the remnants of the tribes of the Quechan, awaiting a new leader. Perhaps he could gather them together and lead them against the white man, even unto death. He turned and trotted gracefully up the hill.

Sheriff Waringer looked down at Print's body lying above the ravine. "There's your escaped prisoner, Ben," he told Harplee, "but I'm afraid my man is in Mexico by now." He pointed toward the haze of the purple hills that formed the Mexican border before he added: "And somehow I'm glad. Come, we better pack the body back to Yuma."

Harplee motioned for the other two guards who had accompanied them to load the dead Negro on one of the sheriff's pack mules. Mounting stiffly on his own horse, Harplee took a long look at the azure hills leading into Mexico. His mind recalled the many trails he had traveled with the Quechan tracker and the dangers they had faced as a team.

He nodded his head slowly and said, "I'm glad this closes the book on Honas Good."

He turned his horse northward toward Yuma.

Author's Note

Since the beginning of this nation, men have been crafting instruments of death and destruction, but of all their inventions none was as effective in molding early American history as Robert Jordan Gatling's gun. A superb weapon for its time, the rapid-fire gun consisted of multibarrels, revolved by a hand crank to fire each chamber in quick succession.

Gatling was able to patent his weapon in November 1862, but governmental authorities moved slowly and the gun was not used until the last phases of the Civil War. Later, the weapon made its appearance at army outposts along the frontier trails where its capability to scatter death rapidly at moving targets soon terrified attacking redskins.

But the weapon really reached its zenith in arousing vibrant fears, when it was issued to prisons where even the most hardened criminals looked askance at the deadly menace. Mounted on light carriage wheels for maneuverability, and with certain other modifications, it became known as a Lowell Battery.

Its presence in the southeast guard tower at Yuma Territorial Prison provided a fearful deterrence to a mass of desperate criminals, hell-bent on escaping from prison.